The
Long
March

The Long March

WILLIAM STYRON
RANDOM HOUSE • NEW YORK

to

Hiram Haydn

The
Long
March

ONE NOON, in the blaze of a cloud-less Carolina summer, what was left of eight dead boys lay strewn about the landscape, among the poison ivy and the pine needles and loblolly saplings. It was not so much as if they had departed this life but as if, sprayed from a hose, they were only shreds of bone, gut, and dangling tissue to which it would have been impossible ever to impute the quality of life, far less the capacity to relinquish it. Of course, though, these had really died quickly, no doubt before the faintest flicker of recognition, of wonder, apprehension, or terror had had time to register in their minds. But the shock, it occurred to Lieutenant Culver, who stood in the shady lee of an ambulance and watched the scene, must have been fantastic to those on the periphery of the explosion, those fifteen or so surviving marines who now lay on the ground beneath blankets, moaning with pain and fright, and who, not more than half an hour before, had been waiting patiently in line for their lunch before the two mortar shells, misfired—how? why? the question already hung with a buzzing, palpable fury in the noontime heat—had plummeted down upon the chow-line and had deadened their ears and senses and had hurled them earthward where they lay now, alive but stricken in a welter of blood and brain, scattered messkits and mashed potatoes, and puddles of melting ice cream. Moments ago in the confusion—just before he had stolen off from the Colonel's side to go behind a tree and get sick—Lieutenant Culver had had a glimpse of a young sweaty face grimed with dust, had heard the boy's voice, astonishing even in that moment of nausea because of its clear, unhysterical tone of explanation: "Major, I tell you I was on the field phone and I tell you as soon as they come out the tube I knew they were short rounds and so I hollered . . ." Of course it had been an accident. But why? He heard the Major shout something, then Culver had heard no more, retching on the leaves with a sound that, for the moment, drowned out the cries and whines of the wounded and the noise of trucks and ambulances crashing up through the underbrush.

It was not that he had a weak stomach or that he was unacquainted with carnage that allowed him to lose control. If anything, he prided himself on his stomach, and as for blood he had seen a lot spilled on Okinawa and had himself (although through no act of valor whatever) received a shrapnel wound —in the buttocks, a matter which even in retrospect, as he had often been forced to remind his wife, possessed no elements of comedy at all. In this case it was simply that on the one hand he himself had been shocked. The sight of death was the sort of thing which in wartime is expected, which one protects oneself against, and which is finally excused or at least ignored, in the same way that a beggar is ignored, or a head cold, or a social problem. But in training here in the States in peacetime (or what, this sweltering summer in the early 1950s, passed as peacetime) one had felt no particular need for that type of self-defense, and the slick nude litter of intestine and shattered blue bones, among which forks and spoons peeked out like so many pathetic metal flowers, made a crazy, insulting impact at Culver's belly, like the blow of a fist. And on the other hand (and the pulsing ache at his brow now as he vomited helplessly onto his shoes lent confirmation to what he'd been trying to deny to himself for months): he was too old, he was no longer an eager kid just out of Quantico with a knife between his teeth. He was almost thirty, he was old, and he was afraid.

Lieutenant Culver had been called back to the marines early that spring. When, one Saturday morning, his wife had thrown the brown envelope containing his orders onto the bed where he lay sleeping, he experienced an odd distress which kept him wandering about,

baffled and mumbling to himself, for days.
Like most of his fellow reserves he had retained his commission after the last war. It
was an insouciant gesture which he had assumed would in some way benefit him in case
of an all-out conflict, say, thirty years hence,
but one which made no provisions for such an
eventuality as a police action in Korea. It
had all come much too soon and Culver had
felt weirdly as if he had fallen asleep in
some barracks in 1945 and had awakened in
a half-dozen years or so to find that the intervening freedom, growth, and serenity had
been only a glorious if somewhat prolonged
dream. A flood of protest had welled up in
him, for he had put the idea of war out of his
mind entirely, and the brief years since Okinawa had been the richest of his life. They
had produced, among lesser things, a loving,
tenderly passionate wife who had passed on
to their little girl both some of her gentle
nature and her wealth of butter-colored hair;
a law degree, the fruits of which he had just
begun to realize, even though still somewhat
impecuniously, as one of the brightest juniors
in a good New York law firm; a friendly

beagle named Howard whom he took for hikes in Washington Square; a cat, whom he did not deign to call by name, and despised; and a record-player that played Haydn, Mozart and Bach.

Up until the day that his orders came— the day that he tried to forget and the one that Betsy, his wife, soon bitterly referred to as "the day the roof fell in"—they had been living in a roomy walk-up in the Village and experiencing the prosaic contentment that comes from eating properly, indulging themselves with fair moderation in the pleasures of the city, and watching the growth of a child. This is not to say that they were either smug or dull. They had a bright circle of friends, mostly young lawyers and newspapermen and doctors and their wives. There were parties and occasional week ends in the country, where everyone became frankly drunk. There were the usual household skirmishes, too, but these were infrequent and petered out quickly. Both of them were too sensible to allow some domestic misdemeanor to develop into anything horrible; they were well adjusted and each of them found it easy to admit, long after the honeymoon, that they were deeply in love. Months later at camp, ensnared futilely in the coils of some administrative flypaper, Culver would find himself gazing up from his work and out across the smoky hot barrens of pine and sand, relieving his vast boredom in a daydream of that vanished simplicity and charm. His mind seemed to drift toward one recurrent vision. This was of the afternoons in winter when— bundled to the ears, the baby-carriage joggling bravely in the van and the melancholy beagle scampering at their heels—they took their Sunday stroll. On such days the city, its frantic heartbeat quieted and clothed in the sooty white tatters of a recent snow, seemed to have an Old World calm, and the people that passed them in the twilight appeared to be, like themselves, pink-cheeked and contented, no matter what crimson alarms flowered at the newsstands or what evil rumors sounded from distant radios. For Culver the waning Sunday light had not spelled out the promise of Monday morning's gloom but of Monday's challenge—and this was not because he was a go-getter but because he was

happy. He was happy to walk through the
chill and leafless dusk with his wife and his
child and his dog. And he was happy to re-
turn home to warmth and peanut butter and
liverwurst, to the familiar delight of the
baby's good-night embrace, to the droll combat between beagle and cat, to music before
sleep. Sometimes in these reveries Culver
thought that it was the music, more than anything, which provided the key, and he recalled himself at a time which already
seemed dark ages ago, surrounded by beer
cans and attuned, in the nostalgic air of a
winter evening, to some passage from some
forgotten Haydn. It was one happy and as-
cending bar that he remembered, a dozen
bright notes through which he passed in memory to an earlier, untroubled day at the end
of childhood. There, like tumbling flowers
against the sunny grass, their motions as nim-
ble as the music itself, two lovely little girls
played tennis, called to him voicelessly, as in
a dream, and waved their arms.

The sordid little town outside the camp
possessed the horror of recognition, for Culver had been there before. They left the baby

with a sister and headed South where, on the outskirts of the town, they found a cramped room in a tourist cabin. They were there for two weeks. They searched vainly for a place to live, there was no more room at the camp. They turned away from bleak cell-like rooms offered at five times their value, were shown huts and chicken-coops by characters whose bland country faces could not hide the sparkle, in their calculating eyes, of venal lust. The aging proprietress of the tourist camp was a scold and a cheat. And so they finally gave up. Betsy went home. He kissed her good-by late one rainy afternoon in the bus station, surrounded by a horde of marines and by cheap suitcases and fallen candy wrappers and the sound of fretful children— all of the unlovely mementoes, so nightmarishly familiar, of leave-taking and of anxiety. Of war. He felt her tears against his cheek. It had been an evil day, and the rain that streamed against the windows, blurring a distant frieze of gaunt gray pines, had seemed to nag with both remembrance and foreboding—of tropic seas, storm-swept distances and strange coasts.

II

He had heard the explosion himself. They
had been eating at their own chow-line in a
command post set up in a grove of trees, when
the noise came from off to the right, distant
enough but still too close: a twin quick earth-
shaking sound—*crump crump*. Then seconds
later in the still of noon when even the birds
had become quiet and only a few murmured
voices disturbed the concentration of eating,
a shudder had passed through the surrounding underbrush, like a faint hot wind. It was
premonitory, perhaps, but still no one knew.
The leaves rustled, ceased, and Culver had
looked up from where he squatted against a
tree to see fifty scattered faces peering toward the noise, their knives and forks sus-
pended. Then from the galley among the trees
a clatter broke the silence, a falling pan or
kettle, and someone laughed, and the Colonel,
sitting nearby, had said to the Major—what
had he said? Culver couldn't remember, yet
there had been something uneasy in his tone,
even then, before anyone had known, and at

least ten minutes before the radio corporal, a tobacco-chewing clown from Oklahoma named Hobbs, came trotting up brushing crumbs from his mouth, a message book clutched in one fat paw. He was popular in battalion headquarters, one of those favored men who, through some simplicity or artlessness of nature, can manage a profane familiarity which in another would be insubordinate; the look of concern on his clown's face, usually so whimsical, communicated an added dread.

"I gotta flash red from Plumbob, Colonel, and it ain't no problem emergency. All hell's broke loose over in Third Battalion. They dropped in some short rounds on a chow-line and they want corpsmen and a doctor and the chaplain. Jesus, you should hear 'em down there."

The Colonel had said nothing at first. The brief flicker of uneasiness in his eyes had fled, and when he put down his messkit and looked up at Hobbs it was only to wipe his hands on his handkerchief and squint casually into the sun, as if he were receiving the most routine of messages. It was absolutely typical of the man, Culver reflected. Too habitual to be an act yet still somehow too faintly self-conscious to be entirely natural, how many years and what strange interior struggle had gone into the perfection of such a gesture? It was good, Grade-A Templeton, perhaps not a distinctly top-notch perform-ance but certainly, from where the critic Cul-ver sat, deserving of applause: the frail, lit-tle-boned, almost pretty face peering upward with a look of attitudinized contemplation; the pensive bulge of tongue sliding inside the rim of one tanned cheek to gouge out some particle of food; small hands working calmly in the folds of the handkerchief—surely all this was more final, more commanding than the arrogant loud mastery of a Booth, more like the skill of Bernhardt, who could cow men by the mystery of her smallest twitch. Perhaps fifteen seconds passed before he spoke. Culver became irritated—at his own suspense, throbbing inside him like a heart-beat, and at the awesome silence which, as if upon order, had fallen over the group of five, detached from the bustle of the rest of the command post: the Colonel; Hobbs; Major

Lawrence, the executive officer, now gazing at the Colonel with moist underlip and deferential anxiety; Captain Mannix; himself. Back off in the bushes a mockingbird commenced a shrill rippling chant and far away, amidst the depth of the silence, there seemed to be a single faint and terrible scream. Hobbs spat an auburn gob of tobacco-juice into the sand, and the Colonel spoke: "Let me have that radio, Hobbs, and get me Plumbob One," he said evenly, and then with no change of tone to the Major: "Billy, send a runner over for Doc Patterson and you two get down there with the chaplain. Take my jeep. Tell the Doc to detach all his corpsmen. And you'd better chop-chop."

The Major scrambled to his feet. He was youthful and handsome, a fine marine in his polished boots, his immaculate dungarees—donned freshly clean, Culver had observed, that morning. He was of the handsomeness preferred by other military men—regular features, clean-cut, rather athletic—but there was a trace of peacetime fleshiness in his cheeks which often lent to the corners of his mouth a sort of petulance, so that every now and again, his young uncomplicated face in deep concentration over some operations map or training schedule or order, he looked like a spoiled and arrogant baby of five. "Aye-aye, sir," he said and bent over the Colonel, bestowing upon him that third-person flattery which to Culver seemed perilously close to bootlicking and was thought to be considerably out of date, especially among the reserves. "Does the Colonel want us to run our own problem as ordered, sir?" He was a regular.

Templeton took the headset from Hobbs, who lowered the radio down beside him in the sand. "Yeah, Billy," he said, without looking up, "yeah, that'll be all right. We'll run her on time. Tell O'Leary to tell all companies to push off at thirteen-hundred."

"Aye-aye, sir." And the Major, boots sparkling, was off in a puff of pine needles and dust.

"Jesus," Mannix said. He put down his messkit and nudged Culver in the ribs. Captain Mannix, the commanding officer of headquarters company, was Culver's friend and, for five months, his closest one. He was a dark heavy-set Jew from Brooklyn, Culver's age and a reserve, too, who had had to sell his radio store and leave his wife and two children at home. He had a disgruntled sense of humor which often seemed to bring a spark of relief not just to his own, but to Culver's, feeling of futility and isolation. Mannix was a bitter man and, in his bitterness, sometimes recklessly vocal. He had long ago given up genteel accents, and spoke like a marine. It was easier, he maintained. "Je-*sus*," he whispered again, too loud, "what'll Congress do about this? Look at Billy chop-chop."

Culver said nothing. His tension eased off a bit, and he looked around him. The news had not seemed yet to have spread around the command post; the men began to get up and walk to the chow-line to clean their mess-gear, strolled back beneath the trees and flopped down, heads against their packs, for a moment's nap. The Colonel spoke in an easy, confidential voice with the other battalion commander: the casualties were confined, Culver gathered, to that outfit. It was a battalion made up mostly of young reserves and it was one in which, he suddenly thanked

God, he knew no one. Then he heard the
Colonel go on calmly—to promise more aid,
to promise to come down himself, shortly.
"Does it look rough, Luke?" Culver heard
him say, "Hold on tight, Luke boy"—all in
the cool and leisurely, almost bored, tones of
a man to whom the greatest embarrassment
would be a show of emotion, and to whom,
because of this quality, had been given, in
the midst of some strained and violent combat
situation long ago, the name "Old Rocky."
He was not yet forty-five, yet the adjective
"old" applied, for there was a gray sheen in
his hair and a bemused, unshakable look in
his tranquil eyes that made him seem, like
certain young ecclesiastics, prematurely aged
and perhaps even wise. Culver saw him put
the headset down and get up, walking off toward the operations tent with a springy, slim-
hipped, boyish stride, calling out over his
shoulder as he went: "Mannix." Simply that:
Mannix. A voice neither harsh nor peremp-
tory nor, on the other hand, particularly
gentle. It was merely a voice which expected
to be obeyed, and Culver felt Mannix's big
weight against him as the Captain put a hand

on his shoulder and pried himself up from the ground, muttering, "Jesus, lemme digest a bit, Jack."

Mannix despised the Colonel. Yet, Culver thought, as the Captain hulked stiff-kneed behind the Colonel and disappeared after him into the operations tent, Mannix despised everything about the Marine Corps. In this attitude he was like nearly all the reserves, it was true, but Mannix was more noisily frank in regard to his position. He detested Templeton not because of any slight or injustice, but because Templeton was a lieutenant colonel, because he was a regular, and because he possessed over Mannix—after six years of freedom—an absolute and unquestioned authority. Mannix would have hated any battalion commander, had he the benignity of Santa Claus, and Culver, listening to Mannix's frequently comical but often too audible complaints, as just now, was kept in a constant state of mild suspense—half amusement, half horror. Culver settled himself against the tree. Apparently there was nothing, for the moment at least, that he could do. Above him an airplane droned through the stillness. A truck grumbled across the clearing, carrying a group of languid hospital corpsmen, was gone; around him the men lay against their packs in crumpled attitudes of sleep. A heavy drowsiness came over him, and he let his eyes slide closed. Suddenly he yearned, with all of the hunger of a schoolboy in a classroom on a May afternoon, to be able to collapse into slumber. For the three days they had been on the problem he had averaged only four hours of sleep a night—almost none last night—and gratefully he knew he'd be able to sleep this evening. He began to doze, dreaming fitfully of home, of white cottages, of a summer by the sea. *Long walk tonight.* And his eyes snapped open then —on what seemed to be the repeated echo, from afar, of that faint anguished shriek he had heard before—in the horrid remembrance that there would be no sleep tonight. For anyone at all. Only a few seconds had passed.

"Long walk tonight," the voice repeated. Culver stared upward through a dazzling patchwork of leaves and light to see the broad pink face of Sergeant O'Leary, smiling down.

"Christ, O'Leary," he said, "don't remind me."

The Sergeant, still grinning, gestured with his shoulder in the direction of the operations tent. "The Colonel's really got a wild hair, ain't he?" He chuckled and reached down and clutched one of his feet, with an elaborate groan.

Culver abruptly felt cloaked in a gloom that was almost tangible, and he was in no mood to laugh. "You'll be really holding that foot tomorrow morning," he said, "and that's no joke."

The grin persisted. "Ah, Mister Culver," O'Leary said, "don't take it so hard. It's just a little walk through the night. It'll be over before you know it." He paused, prodding with his toe at the pine needles. "Say," he went on, "what's this I heard about some short rounds down in Third Batt?"

"I don't know from nothing, O'Leary. I just read the papers." Another truck came by, loaded with corpsmen, followed by a jeep in which sat the helmeted Major Lawrence, a look of sulky arrogance on his face, his arms folded at his chest like a legionnaire riding through a conquered city. "But from what I understand," Culver went on, turning back, "quite a few guys got hurt."

"That's tough," O'Leary said. "I'll bet you they were using that old stuff they've had stored on Guam ever since '45. Jesus, you'd think they'd have better sense. Why, I seen those shells stacked up high as a man out there just last year, getting rained on every day and getting the jungle rot and Jesus, they put tarps over 'em but five years is one hell of a long time to let 81-shells lay around. I remember once . . ." Culver let him talk, without hearing the words, and drowsed. O'Leary was an old-timer (though only a few years older than Culver), a regular who had just signed over for four more years, and it was impossible to dislike him. On Guadalcanal he had been only a youngster, but in the intervening years the Marine Corps had molded him—perhaps by his own unconscious choice—in its image, and he had become as inextricably grafted to the system as any piece of flesh surgically laid on to arm or thigh. There was great heartiness and warmth in him but at the same time he performed all infantry jobs with a devoted, methodical competence. He could say sarcastically, "The Colonel's really got a wild hair, ain't he?" but shrug his shoulders and grin, and by that ambivalent gesture sum up an attitude which only a professional soldier could logically retain: I doubt the Colonel's judgment a little, but I will willingly do what he says. He also shared with Hobbs, the radioman, some sort of immunity. And thus it had been last night, Culver recalled, that upon the Colonel's announcement about this evening's forced march—which was to take thirteen hours and extend the nearly thirty-six miles back to the main base—O'Leary had been able to give a long, audible, incredulous whistle, right in the Colonel's face, and elicit from the Colonel an indulgent smile; whereas in the same blackout tent and at virtually the same instant Mannix had murmured, "Thirty-six miles, Jesus Christ," in a tone, however, laden with no more disbelief or no more pain than O'Leary's whistle, and

Culver had seen the Colonel's smile vanish, replaced on the fragile little face by a subtle, delicate shadow of irritation.

"You think that's too long?" the Colonel had said to Mannix then, turning slightly. There had been no hostility in his voice, or even reproof; it had, in fact, seemed merely a question candidly stated—although this might have been because two enlisted men had been in the tent, O'Leary, and some wizened, anonymous little private shivering over the radio. It was midsummer, but nights out in the swamps were fiercely, illogically cold, and from where they had set up the operations tent that evening—on a tiny patch of squashy marshland—the dampness seemed to ooze up and around them, clutching their bones in a chill which extra sweaters and field jackets and sweatshirts could not dislodge. A single kerosene pressure-lamp dangled from overhead—roaring like a pint-sized, encapsuled hurricane; it furnished the only light in the tent, and the negligible solace of a candlelike heat. It had the stark, desperate, manufactured quality of the light one imagines in an execution chamber; under it the Colonel's face, in absolute repose as he stared down for a brief, silent instant and awaited Mannix's reply, looked like that of a mannequin, chalky, exquisite, solitary beneath a store-window glare.

"No, sir," Mannix said. He had recovered quickly. He peered up at the Colonel from his camp stool, expressionless. "No, sir," he repeated, "I don't think it's too long, but it's certainly going to be some hike."

The Colonel did something with his lips. It seemed to be a smile. He said nothing—bemused and mystifying—wearing the enigma of the moment like a cape. In the silence the tempestuous little lamp boiled and raged; far off in the swamp somewhere a mortar flare flew up with a short, sharp crack. O'Leary broke the quietness in the tent with a loud sneeze, followed, almost like a prolongation of the sneeze, by a chuckle, and said: "Oh boy, Colonel, there're gonna be some sore feet Saturday morning."

The Colonel didn't answer. He hooked his thumbs in his belt. He turned to the Major, who was brooding upward from the field desk, cheeks propped against his hands. "I was sitting in my tent a while ago, Billy," the Colonel said, "and I got to thinking. I got to thinking about a lot of things. I got to thinking about the Battalion. I said to myself, 'How's the Battalion doing?' I mean, 'What kind of an outfit do I have here? Is it in good combat shape? If we were to meet an Aggressor enemy tomorrow would we come out all right?' Those were the queries I posed to myself. Then I tried to formulate an answer." He paused, his eyes luminous and his lips twisted in a wry, contemplative smile as if he were indeed, again, struggling with the weight of the questions to which he had addressed himself. The Major was absorbed; he looked up at Templeton with an intent baby-blue gaze and parted mouth, upon which, against a pink cleft of the lower lip, there glittered a bead of saliva. "Reluctantly," the Colonel went on slowly, "reluctantly, I came to this conclusion: the Battalion's been doping off." He paused again. "Doping off. Especially," he said, turning briefly toward Mannix with a thin smile, "a certain component unit known as Headquarters and Service Company." He leaned back on the camp stool and slowly caressed the pewter-colored surface of his hair. "I decided a little walk might be in order for tomorrow night, after we secure the problem. Instead of going back to the base on the trucks. What do you think, Billy?"

"I think that's an excellent idea, sir. An excellent idea. In fact I've been meaning to suggest something like that to the Colonel for quite some time. As a means of inculcating a sort of group *esprit.*"

"It's what they need, Billy."

"Full marching order, sir?" O'Leary put in seriously.

"No, that'd be a little rough."

"Aaa-h," O'Leary said, relieved.

Suddenly Culver heard Mannix's voice: "Even so—"

"Even so, what?" the Colonel interrupted. Again, the voice was not hostile, only anticipatory, as if it already held the answer to whatever Mannix might ask or suggest.

"Well, even so, Colonel," Mannix went on mildly, while Culver, suddenly taut and concerned, held his breath, "even without packs thirty-six miles is a long way for anybody, much less for guys who've gone soft for the past five or six years. I'll admit my company isn't the hottest outfit in the world, but most of them are reserves—"

"Wait a minute, Captain, wait a minute," the Colonel said. Once more the voice—as cool and as level as the marshy ground upon which they were sitting—carefully skirted any tone of reproach and was merely explicit: "I don't want you to think I'm taking it out on the Battalion merely because of you, or rather H & S Company. But they aren't reserves. They're *marines. Comprend?*" He arose from the chair. "I think," he went on flatly, almost gently, "that there's one thing that we are all tending to overlook these days. We've been trying to differentiate too closely between two particular bodies of men that make up the Marine Corps. Technically it's true that a lot of these new men are reserves—that is, they have an 'R' affixed at the end of the 'USMC.' But it's only a technical difference, you see. Because first and foremost they're *marines*. I don't want my marines doping off. They're going to *act* like marines. They're going to be *fit*. If they

meet an Aggressor enemy next week they
might have to march a long, long way. And
that's what I want this hike to teach them.
Comprend?" He made what could pass for
the token of a smile and laid his hand easily
and for a lingering second on Mannix's shoulder, in a sort of half-gesture of conciliation,
understanding—something—it was hard to
tell. It was an odd picture because from
where he sat Culver was the only one in the
tent who could see, at the same instant, both
of their expressions. In the morbid, comfortless light they were like classical Greek
masks, made of chrome or tin, reflecting an
almost theatrical disharmony: the Colonel's
fleeting grin sculpted cleanly and prettily in
the unshadowed air above the Captain's dark-
ened, downcast face where, for a flicker of
a second, something outraged and agonized
was swiftly graven and swiftly scratched out.
The Colonel's smile was not complacent or
unfriendly. It was not so much as if he had
achieved a triumph but merely equilibrium,
had returned once more to that devout, ordered state of communion which the Captain's words had ever so briefly disturbed. At

that moment Culver almost liked the Colonel, in some negative way which had nothing to do with affection, but to which "respect," though he hated the word, was the nearest approach. At least it was an honest smile, no matter how faint. It was the expression of a man who might be fatuous and a ham of sorts, but was not himself evil or unjust—a man who would like to overhear some sergeant say, "He keeps a tight outfit, but he's straight." In men like Templeton all emotions—all smiles, all anger—emanated from a priestlike, religious fervor, throbbing inwardly with the cadence of parades and booted footfalls. By that passion rebels are ordered into quick damnation but simple doubters sometimes find indulgence— depending upon the priest, who may be one inclined toward mercy, or who is one ever rapt in some litany of punishment and court-martial. The Colonel was devout but inclined toward mercy. He was not a tyrant, and his smile was a sign that the Captain's doubts were forgiven, probably even forgotten. But only Culver had seen the Captain's face: a quick look of both fury and suffering, like the

tragic Greek mask, or a shackled slave. Then
Mannix flushed. "Yes, sir," he said.

The Colonel walked toward the door. He
seemed already to have put the incident out
of his mind. "Culver," he said, "if you can
ever make radio contact with Able Company
tell them to push off at 0600. If you can't,
send a runner down before dawn to see if
they've got the word." He gave the side of
his thigh a rather self-conscious, gratuitous
slap. "Well, good night."

There was a chorus of "Good night, sirs,"
and then the Major went out, too, trailed by
O'Leary. Culver looked at his watch: it was
nearly three o'clock.

Mannix looked up. "You going to try and
get some sleep, Tom?"

"I've tried. It's too cold. Anyway, I've
got to take over the radio watch from Junior
here. What's your name, fellow?"

The boy at the radio looked up with a
start, trembling with the cold. "McDonald,
sir." He was very young, with pimples and a
sweet earnest expression; he had obviously
just come from boot camp, for he had prac-
tically no hair.

"Well, you can shove off and get some sleep, if you can find a nice warm pile of pine needles somewhere." The boy sleepily put down his earphones and went out, fastening the blackout flap behind him.

"I've tried," Culver repeated, "but I just can't get used to sleeping on the ground any more. I'm getting old and rheumatic. Anyway, the Old Rock was in here for about two hours before you came, using up my sack time while he told the Major and O'Leary and me all about his Shanghai days."

"He's a son of a bitch." Mannix morosely cupped his chin in his hands, blinking into space, at the bare canvas wall. He was chewing on the butt of a cigar. The glare seemed to accentuate a flat Mongoloid cast in his face; he looked surly and tough and utterly exhausted. Shivering, he pulled his field jacket closer around his neck, and then, as Culver watched, his face broke out into the comical, exasperated smile which always heralded his bitterest moments of outrage —at the Marine Corps, at the system, at their helpless plight, the state of the world—tirades which, in their unqualified cynicism, would have been intolerable were they not always delivered with such gusto and humor and a kind of grisly delight. "Thirty . . . six . . . *miles*," he said slowly, his eyes alive and glistening, *"thirty . . . six . . . miles!* Christ on a crutch! Do you realize how far that is? Why that's as far as it is from Grand Central to Stamford, Connecticut! Why, man, I haven't walked a hundred consecutive yards since 1945. I couldn't go thirty-six miles if I were sliding downhill the whole way on a sled. And a *forced* march, mind you. You just don't stroll along, you know. That's like running. That's a regulation two-and-a-half miles per hour with only a ten-minute break each hour. So H & S Company is fouled up. So maybe it is. He can't take green troops like these and do that. After a couple of seven- or ten- or fifteen-mile conditioning hikes, maybe so. If they were young. And rested. Barracks-fresh. But this silly son of a bitch is going to have all these tired, flabby old men flapping around on the ground like a bunch of fish after the first two miles. Christ on a frigging crutch!"

"He's not a bad guy, Al," Culver said,

"he's just a regular. Shot in the ass with the Corps. A bit off his nut, like all of them."

But Mannix had made the march seem menacing, there was no doubt about that, and Culver—who for the moment had been regarding the hike as a sort of careless abstraction, a prolonged evening's stroll—felt a solid dread creep into his bones, along with the chill of the night. Involuntarily, he shuddered. He felt suddenly unreal and disoriented, as if through some curious second sight or seventh sense his surroundings had shifted, ever so imperceptibly, into another dimension of space and time. Perhaps he was just so tired. Freezing marsh and grass instead of wood beneath his feet, the preposterous cold in the midst of summer, Mannix's huge distorted shadow cast brutishly against the impermeable walls by a lantern so sinister that its raging noise had the sound of a typhoon at sea—all these, just for an instant, did indeed contrive to make him feel as if they were adrift at sea in a dazzling, windowless box, ignorant of direction or of any points of the globe, and with no way of telling. What he had had for the last years—wife and child and home—seemed to have existed in the infinite past or, dreamlike again, never at all, and what he had done yesterday and the day before, moving wearily with this tent from one strange thicket to a stranger swamp and on to the green depths of some even stranger ravine, had no sequence, like the dream of a man delirious with fever. All time and space seemed for a moment to be enclosed within the tent, itself unmoored and unhelmed upon a dark and compassless ocean.

And although Mannix was close by, he felt profoundly alone. Something that had happened that evening—something Mannix had said, or suggested, perhaps not even that, but only a fleeting look in the Captain's face, the old compressed look of torment mingled with seething outrage—something that evening, without a doubt, had added to the great load of his loneliness an almost intolerable burden. And that burden was simply an anxiety, nameless for the moment and therefore the more menacing. It was not merely the prospect of the hike. Exhaustion had just made him vulnerable to a million shaky, anony-

mous fears—fears which he might have re-
sisted had he felt strong and refreshed, or
younger. His age was showing badly. All this
would have been easy at twenty-three. But he
was thirty, and seventy-two virtually sleepless
hours had left him feeling bushed and de-
feated. And there was another subtle difference he felt about his advanced age—a new
awakening, an awareness—and therein lay
the reason for his fears.

It was simply that after six years of an
ordered and sympathetic life—made the
more placid by the fact that he had assumed
he had put war forever behind him—it was a
shock almost mystically horrifying, in its unreality, to find himself in this new world of
frigid nights and blazing noons, of disorder
and movement and fanciful pursuit. He was
insecure and uprooted and the prey of many
fears. Not for days but for weeks, it seemed,
the battalion had been on the trail of an in-
visible enemy who always eluded them and
kept them pressing on—across swamps and
blasted fields and past indolent, alien
streams. This enemy was labeled Aggressor,
on maps brightly spattered with arrows and

symbolic tanks and guns, but although there was no sign of his aggression he fled them nonetheless and they pushed the sinister chase, sending up shells and flares as they went. Five hours' pause, five hours in a tent somewhere, lent to the surrounding grove of trees a warm, homelike familiarity that was almost like permanence, and he left each command post feeling lonely and uprooted, as they pushed on after the spectral foe into the infinite strangeness of another swamp or grove. Fatigue pressed down on his shoulders like strong hands, and he awoke in the morning feeling weary, if he ever slept at all. Since their constant movement made the sunlight come from ever-shifting points of the compass, he was often never quite sure—in his steady exhaustion—whether it was morning or afternoon. The displacement and the confusion filled him with an anxiety which would not have been possible six years before, and increased his fatigue. The tent itself, in its tiny, momentary permanence, might have had all of the appeal of the home which he so desperately hungered for, had it not been so cold, and had it not seemed, as he sat there suddenly shivering with fear, so much more like a coffin instead.

Then it occurred to him that he was actually terrified of the march, of the thirty-six miles: not because of the length—which was beyond comprehension—but because he was sure he'd not be able to make it. The contagion of Mannix's fear had touched him. And he wondered then if Mannix's fear had been like his own: that no matter what his hatred of the system, of the Marine Corps, might be, some instilled, twisted pride would make him walk until he dropped, and his fear was not of the hike itself, but of dropping. He looked up at Mannix and said, "Do you think you can make it, Al?"

Mannix heavily slapped his knee. He seemed not to have heard the question. The giddy sensation passed, and Culver got up to warm his hands at the lamp.

"I'll bet if Regiment or Division got wind of this they'd lower the boom on the bastard," Mannix said.

"They have already. They said fine."

"What do you mean? How do you know?"

"He said so, before you came in. He radioed to the base for permission, or so he said."

"The bastard."

"He wouldn't dare without it," Culver
said. "What I can't figure out is why Regiment gave him the O.K. on it."

"The swine. The little swine. It's not on
account of H & S Company. You know that.
It's because it's an exploit. He wants to be
known as a tough guy, a boondocker."

"There's one consolation, though," said
Culver, after a pause, "if it'll help you any."

"What, for God's sake?"

"Old Rocky, or whatever they call him, is
going to hike along, too."

"You think so?" Mannix said doubtfully.

"I know so. So do you. He wouldn't dare
not push along with his men."

Mannix was silent for a moment. Then he
said viciously, as if obsessed with the idea
that no act of Templeton's could remain un-
tainted by a prime and calculated evil: "But
the son of a bitch! He's made for that sort of
thing. He's been running around the boondocks for six years getting in shape while
sane people like you and me were home living like humans and taking it easy. Billy

Lawrence, too. They're both gung ho. These fat civilians can't take that sort of thing. My God! Hobbs! Look at that radioman, Hobbs. That guy's going to keel over two minutes out—" He rose suddenly to his feet and stretched, his voice stifled by the long, indrawn breath of a yawn. "Aaa-h, fuck it. I'm going to hit the sack."

"Why don't you?"

"Fine bed. A poncho in a pile of poison ivy. My ass looks like a chessboard from chigger bites. Jesus, if Mimi could see me now." He paused and pawed at his red-rimmed eyes. "Yeah," he said, blinking at his watch, "I think I will." He slapped Culver on the back, without much heartiness. "I'll see you tomorrow, sport. Stay loose." Then he lumbered from the tent, mumbling something: *be in for fifty years.*

Culver turned away from the lamp. He sat down at the field desk, strapping a black garland of wires and earphones around his skull. The wild, lost wail of the radio signal struck his ears, mingling with the roar, much closer now, of the lamp; alone as he was, the chill and cramped universe of the tent seemed

made for no one more competent than a blind
midget, and was on the verge of bursting with
a swollen obbligato of demented sounds. He
felt almost sick with the need for sleep and,
with the earphones still around his head, he
thrust his face into his arms on the field desk.
There was nothing on the radio except the
signal; far off in the swamp the companies
were sleeping wretchedly in scattered squads
and platoons, tumbled about in the cold and
the dark, and dreaming fitful dreams. The
radios were dead everywhere, except for their
signals: a crazy, tortured multitude of wails
on which his imagination played in exhaustion. They seemed like the cries of souls in
the anguish of hell, if he concentrated closely
enough, shrill cracklings, whines, barks and
shrieks—a whole jungle full of noise an inch
from his eardrum and across which, like a
thread of insanity, was strung the single faint
fluting of a dance-band clarinet—blown in
from Florida or New York, someplace beyond reckoning. His universe now seemed
even more contained: not merely by the tiny
space of the tent, but by the almost tangible
fact of sound. And it was impossible to sleep.

Besides, something weighed heavily on his mind; there was something he had forgotten, something he was supposed to do . . .

Then suddenly he remembered the Colonel's instructions. He cleared his throat and spoke drowsily into the mouthpiece, his head still resting against his arms. "This is Bundle Three calling Bundle Able. This is Bundle Three calling Bundle Able. This is Bundle Three calling Bundle Able. Do you hear me? Over . . ." He paused for a moment, waiting. There was no answer. He repeated: "This is Bundle Three calling Bundle Able, this is Bundle Three calling Bundle Able, this is. . . ." And he snapped abruptly erect, thinking of Mannix, thinking: to hell with it: simply because the words made him feel juvenile and absurd, as if he were reciting Mother Goose.

He *would* stay awake. And he thought of Mannix. Because Mannix would laugh. Mannix appreciated the idiocy of those radio words, just as in his own crazy way he managed to put his finger on anything which might represent a symbol of their predicament. Like the radio code. He had a violent contempt for the gibberish, the boy-scout passwords which replaced ordinary conversation in the military world. To Mannix they were all part of the secret language of a group of morons, morons who had been made irresponsibly and dangerously clever. He had despised the other side, also—the sweat, the exertion, and the final danger. It had been he, too, who had said, "None of this Hemingway crap for me, Jack"; he was nobody's lousy hero, and he'd get out of this outfit some way. Yet, Culver speculated, who really was a hero anyway, any more? Mannix's disavowal of faith put him automatically out of the hero category, in the classical sense, yet if suffering was part of the hero's role, wasn't Mannix as heroic as any? On his shoulder there was a raw, deeply dented, livid scar, made the more conspicuous and, for that matter, more ugly, by the fact that its evil slick surface only emphasized the burly growth of hair around it. There were smaller scars all over his body. About them Mannix was neither proud nor modest, but just frank, and once while they were showering down after a day in the field, Mannix told him how he had gotten the scars, one day on Peleliu. "I was a buck sergeant then. I got pinned down in a shell hole out in front of my platoon. Christ knows how I got there but I remember there was a telephone in the hole and—whammo! —the Nips began laying in mortar fire on the area and I got a piece right here." He pointed to a shiny, triangular groove just above his knee. "I remember grabbing that phone and hollering for them to for Christ's sake get the 81s up and knock out that position, but they were slow, Jesus they were slow! The Nips were firing for effect, I guess, because they were coming down like rain and every time one of the goddam things went off I seemed to catch it. All I can remember is hollering into that phone and the rounds going off and the zinging noise that shrapnel made. I hollered for 81s and I caught a piece in my hand. Then I hollered for at least a goddam rifle grenade and I caught a piece in the ass, right here. I hollered for 60s and guns and airplanes. Every time I hollered for something I seemed to catch some steel. Christ, I was scared. And hurting! Jesus Christ, I never hurt so much in my life. Then

I caught this one right here"—he made a comical, contorted gesture, with a bar of soap, over his shoulder—"man, it was lights out then. I remember thinking, 'Al, you've had it,' and just before I passed out I looked down at that telephone. You know, that frigging wire had been blasted right out of sight all that time."

No, perhaps Mannix wasn't a hero, any more than the rest of them, caught up by wars in which, decade by half-decade, the combatant served peonage to the telephone and the radar and the thunderjet—a horde of cunningly designed, and therefore often treacherous, machines. But Mannix had suffered once, that "once" being, in his own words, "once too goddam many, Jack." And his own particular suffering had made him angry, had given him an acute, if cynical, perception about their renewed bondage, and a keen nose for the winds that threatened to blow up out of the oppressive weather of their surroundings and sweep them all into violence. And he made Culver uneasy. His discontent was not merely peevish; it was rocklike and rebellious, and thus this discontent seemed to Culver to be at once brave and somehow full of peril.

He had first seen Mannix the revolutionary five months ago, soon after they had been called back to duty. He hadn't known him then. There were compulsory lectures arranged at first, to acquaint the junior officers with recent developments in what had been called "the new amphibious doctrine." The outlines of these lectures were appallingly familiar: the stuffy auditorium asprawl with bored lieutenants and captains, the brightly lit stage with its magnified charts and graphs, the lantern slides (at which point, when the lights went out, it was possible to sneak a moment's nap, just as in officers' school seven years ago), the parade of majors and colonels with their maps and pointers, and their cruelly tedious, doggedly memorized lectures: the whole scene, with its grave, professorial air, seemed seedily portentous, especially since no one cared, save the majors and colonels, and no one listened. When Culver sat down, during the darkness of a lantern slide, next to the big relaxed mass which he dimly identified as a captain, he noticed that it was snoring. When the lights went up, Mannix still slept on, filling the air around him with a loud, tranquil blubber. Culver aroused him with a nudge. Mannix grumbled something, but then said, "Thanks, Jack." A young colonel had come onto the stage then. He had made many of the lectures that week. He had a curiously thick, throaty voice which would have made him sound like a yokel, except that his words were coolly, almost passionately put, and he bent forward over the lectern with a bleak and solemn attitude—a lean, natty figure with hair cut so close to his head that he appeared to be, from that distance, nearly bald. "An SS man," Mannix whispered, "he's gonna come down here and cut your balls off. You Jewish?" He grinned and collapsed back, forehead against his hand, into quiet slumber. Culver couldn't recall what the colonel talked about: the movement of supplies, logistics, ship-to-shore movement, long-range planning, all abstract and vast, and an ardent glint came to his eyes when he spoke of the "grandiose doctrine" which had been formulated since they, the reserves, had been away. "You bet your life,

Jack," Mannix had whispered out of the shadows then. He seemed to have snapped fully awake and, following the lecture intently, he appeared to address his whispers not to Culver, or the colonel, but to the air. "You bet your life they're grandiose," he said, "even if you don't know what grandiose means. I'll bet you'd sell your soul to be able to drop a bomb on somebody." And then, aping the colonel's instructions to the corporal—one of the enlisted flunkies who, after each lecture, passed out the reams of printed and mimeographed tables and charts and résumés, which everyone promptly, when out of sight, threw away—he whispered in high, throaty, lilting mockery: "Corporal, kindly pass out the atom bombs for inspection." He smacked the arm of his seat, too hard; it could be heard across the auditorium, and heads turned then, but the colonel had not seemed to have noticed. "Jesus," Mannix rumbled furiously, "Jesus Christ almighty," while the colonel droned on, in his countrified voice: "Our group destiny," he said, "amphibiously integrated, from any force thrown against us by Aggressor enemy."

Later—toward the end of that week of lectures, after Mannix had spoken the calm, public manifesto which at least among the reserves had made him famous, and from then on the object of a certain awe, though with a few doubts about his balance, too—Culver had tried to calculate how he had gotten by with it. Perhaps it had to do with his size, his bearing. There was at times a great massive absoluteness in the way he spoke. He was huge, and the complete honesty and candor of his approach seemed to rumble forth, like notes from a sounding board, in direct proportion to his size. He had suffered, too, and this suffering had left a persistent, unwhipped, scornful look in his eyes, almost like a stain, or rather a wound, which spells out its own warning and cautions the unwary to handle this tortured parcel of flesh with care. And he was an enormous man, his carriage was formidable. That skinny, bristle-haired colonel, Culver finally realized, had been taken aback past the point of punishment, or even reprimand, merely because of the towering, unavoidable, physical fact that he was facing not a student or a captain or a subordinate, but a stubborn and passionate man. So it was that, after a lecture on transport of supplies, when the colonel had called Mannix's name at random from a list to answer some generalized, hypothetical question, Mannix had stood up and said merely, "I don't know, sir." A murmur of surprise passed over the auditorium then, for the colonel, early in the hour, had made it plain that he had wanted at least an attempt at an answer—a guess—even though they might be unacquainted with the subject. But Mannix merely said, "I don't know, sir," while the colonel, as if he hadn't heard correctly, rephrased the question with a little tremor of annoyance. There was a moment's silence and men turned around in their seats to look at the author of this defiance. "I don't know, sir," he said again, in a loud but calm voice. "I don't know what my first consideration would be in making a space table like that. I'm an infantry officer. I got an 0302." The colonel's forehead went pink under the glare of the lights. "I stated earlier, Captain, that I wanted some sort of answer. None of you gentlemen is expected to know this subject pat, but you can essay *some kind of an answer.*" Mannix just stood there, solid and huge, blinking at the colonel. "I just have to repeat, sir," he said finally, "that I don't have the faintest idea what my first consideration would be. I never went to cargo-loading school. I'm an 0302. And I'd like to respectfully add, sir, if I might, that there's hardly anybody in this room who knows that answer, either. They've forgotten everything they ever learned seven years ago. Most of them don't even know how to take an M-1 apart. They're too old. They should be home with their family." There was passion in his tone but it was controlled and straightforward—he had managed to keep out of his voice either anger or insolence—and then he fell silent. His words had the quality, the sternness, of an absolute and unequivocal fact, as if they had been some intercession for grace spoken across the heads of a courtroom by a lawyer so quietly convinced of his man's innocence that there was no need for gesticulations or frenzy. The colonel's eyes bulged incredulously at Mannix from across the rows of seats, but in the complete, astounded hush that had followed

he was apparently at a loss for words. A bit
unsteadily, he called out another name and
Mannix sat down, staring stonily ahead.

It had been perhaps a court-martial of-
fense, at least worthy of some reprimand, but
that was all there was to it. Nothing happened, no repercussions, nothing. The thing
had been forgotten; either that, or it had
been stored away in the universal memory of
colonels, where all such incidents are sorted
out for retribution, or are forgotten. Whatever effect it had on the colonel, or whatever
higher, even more important sources got
wind of it, it had its effect on Mannix. And
the result was odd. Far from giving the impression that he had been purged, that he had
blown off excess pressure, he seemed instead
more tense, more embittered, more in need to
scourge something—his own boiling spirit,
authority, anything.

Culver's vision of him at this time was always projected against Heaven's Gate, which
was the name—no doubt ironically supplied
at first by the enlisted men—of the pleasure-
dome ingeniously erected amid a tangle of
alluvial swampland, and for officers only. He

and Mannix lived in rooms next to each other,
in the bachelor quarters upstairs. The entire
area was a playground which had all the
casual opulence of a Riviera resort and
found its focus in the sparkling waters of a
swimming pool, set like an oblong sapphire
amid flowered walks and a fanciful growth
of beach umbrellas. There, at ten minutes
past four each day, Mannix could be found,
his uniform shed in an instant and a gin fizz
in his hand—a sullen, mountainous figure in
a lurid sportshirt, across which a squadron of
monstrous butterflies floated in luminous, un-
military files. Both Mannix and Culver hated
the place—its factitious luxury, its wanton
atmosphere of alcohol and torpid ease and
dances, the vacant professional talk of the
regular officers and the constant teasing pres-
ence of their wives, who were beautiful and
spoke in tender drawls and boldly flaunted at
the wifeless reserves—in a proprietary, At-
lanta-debutante fashion—their lecherous sort
of chastity. The place seemed to offer up, like
a cornucopia, the fruits of boredom, of foot-
lessness and dissolution. It was, in Mannix's
words, like a prison where you could have

anything you wanted except happiness, and
once, in a rare midnight moment when he allowed himself to get drunk, he got paper and
wood together from his room and announced
to Culver in an unsteady but determined voice
that he was going to burn the place down.
Culver held him off, but it was true: they
were bound to the pleasures of the place by
necessity—for there was no place to go for a
hundred miles, even if they had wanted to go
—and therefore out of futility. "Goddam,
it's degrading," Mannix had said, making
use of an adjective which indeed seemed to
sum it all up. "It's like sex now. Or the lack
of it. Now maybe it's all right for a kid to go
without sex, but it's degrading for someone
like me almost thirty to go without making
love for so long. It's simply degrading, that's
all. I'd go for one of these regulars' pigs if it
wasn't for Mimi. . . . This whole mess is
degrading. I know it's my own fault I stayed
in the reserves, Jack, you don't have to tell me
that. I was a nut. I didn't know I was going to
get called out for every frigging interna-
tional incident that came along. But, goddam,
it's degrading"—and with a glum, subdued

gesture he'd down the dregs of his drink—
"it's degrading for a man my age to go
sniffing around on my belly in the boondocks
like a dog. And furthermore—" He looked
scornfully about him, at the glitter and
chrome, at the terrace by the pool where Japa-
nese lanterns hung like a grove of pastel
moons, and a girl's shrill and empty laugh
uncoiled as bright as tinsel through the slug-
gish coastal dusk. It was a silent moment in a
night sprinkled with a dusty multitude of
Southern stars, and the distant bleating saxo-
phone seemed indecisive and sad, like the
nation and the suffocating summer, neither at
peace nor at war. "Furthermore, it's degrading to come out of the field each day and then
be *forced* to go to a night club like this, when
all you want to do is go home to your wife
and family. Goddam, man, I've *gotta* get
out!"

But underneath his rebellion, Culver
finally knew, Mannix—like all of them—was
really resigned. Born into a generation of
conformists, even Mannix (so Culver sensed)
was aware that his gestures were not symbolic, but individual, therefore hopeless,

maybe even absurd, and that he was trapped
like all of them in a predicament which one
personal insurrection could, if anything, only
make worse. "You know," he said once, "I
think I was really afraid just one time last
war." The phrase "last war" had had, itself,
a numb, resigned quality, in its lack of any
particular inflection, like "last week end," or
"last movie I went to see." They had been lying on the beach to which they fled each hot
week end. In that setting of coast and sea and
lugubrious solitude they felt nearly peaceful,
in touch with a tranquil force more important, and more lasting (or so it seemed on
those sunlit afternoons), than war. Mannix
had been, almost for the first time since
Culver had known him, rested and subdued,
and the sound of his voice had been a surprise after long, sun-laden hours of sleep and
silence. "That's the goddam truth," he said
thoughtfully, "I was only afraid once. Really
afraid, I mean. It was at a hotel in San Francisco. I think I really came closer to dying
that night than I ever have in my life. We
were drunk, you see, polluted, all of us. I
think there were five of us, all of us boots

just out of Dago. Kids. We were on the tenth
floor of this hotel and in this room and I believe we were about as drunk as anyone could
get. I remember going in to take a shower in the
bathroom. It was late at night, past midnight,
and after I took this shower, you see, I came
out into the room buck naked. Two of those
drunk guys were waiting for me. They
grabbed me and pushed me toward the window. I was so loaded I couldn't battle. Then
they pushed me out the window and held me
by the heels while I dangled upside-down
buck naked in space, ten floors above the
street." He paused and sucked at a beer can.
"Can you imagine that?" he went on slowly.
"How I felt? I got stone-sober in a second.
Imagine being that high upside-down in space
with two drunks holding onto your heels. I
was heavy, man, just like now, you see. All I
can remember is those teeny-weeny lights below and the tiny little people like ants down
there and those two crazy drunk guys holding
onto my wet slippery ankles, laughing like
hell and trying to decide whether to let go or
not. I just remember the cold wind blowing
on my body and that dark, man, infinite dark-

ness all around me, and my ankles beginning to slip out of their hands. I really saw Death then, and I think that all I could think of was that I was going to fall and smash myself on that hard, hard street below. That those crazy bastards were going to let me fall. I was praying, I guess. I remember the blood rushing to my brain and my ankles slipping, and that awful strange noise. And I was reaching out, man, clutching at thin air. Then I wondered what that noise was, that high loud noise, and then I realized it was me, screaming at the top of my voice, all over San Francisco." He stopped talking then and scuffed at the sand with one calloused heel. "They hauled me up somehow. It was those sober guys—I guess they were sober—the other two. They got me up. But every time I remember that moment a great big cold shudder runs up and down my spine." He chuckled and chewed on his cigar but the laugh was half-hearted and listless, and he dug his elbows into the sand and resumed his quiet, placid gaze toward the horizon. Culver watched him: his bitterness dissolved in the hot salty air, slumped in the sand gazing wistfully out to sea, sun-glassed, hairy-chested, a cigar protruding from his face and a beer can warming in his hand, he seemed no longer the man who could sicken himself with resentment, but relaxed, pliable even, like a huge hairy baby soothed by the wash of elemental tides, ready to receive anything, all, into that great void in his soul which bitterness and rebellion had briefly left vacant—all—the finality of more suffering, or even death. War was in the offing. A promenade of waves, snow-crowned like lovely garlands in the dark hair of girls, swelled eastward toward Africa: past those smoky heights, more eastward still, the horizon seemed to give back repeated echoes of the sea, like far-off thunder, or guns. Culver remembered making a quick, contorted motion in the sand with his body, and being swept by a hot wave of anguish. It was loneliness and homesickness, but it was also fright. Across the rim of his memory two little girls playing on the sunny grass waved to him, were gone, pursued by a shower of uncapturable musical sounds. Mannix's resigned silence fed his loneliness. Suddenly he felt, like Mannix, upturned drunkenly above the abyss, blood rushing to his head, in terror clutching at the substanceless night. . . .

In the noonday light Sergeant O'Leary, his face brightly pink, was still talking. Culver snapped awake with a start. O'Leary grinned down at him—"Damn, Lieutenant, you're gonna crap out tonight if you're that tired now"—and Culver struggled for speech; time seemed to have unspooled past him in a great spiral, and for an instant—his mind still grappling with the memory of a hurried, chaotic nightmare—he was unable to tell where he was. He had the feeling that it should be the night before, and that he was still in the tent. "Did I go to sleep, O'Leary?" he said, blinking upward.

"Yes, sir," O'Leary said, and chuckled, "you sure did."

"How long?"

"Oh, just a second."

"Christ, I *am* tired. I dreamt it was last night," Culver said. He got to his feet. A truck moved through the clearing in a cloud of dust. There seemed to be new activity in the command post, and new confusion. Culver and O'Leary turned together then toward the operations tent; the Colonel had come out and was striding toward them, followed by Mannix.

"Culver, get your jeep and driver," he said, walking toward the road, not looking up. His voice was briskly matter-of-fact; he strode past them with short, choppy steps and the swagger stick in his hand made a quick tattoo, *slap-slap*-slapping against his dungaree pants. "I want you and Captain Mannix to go with me down to Third Batt. See if we can help." His voice faded; Mannix trailed behind him, saying nothing, but his face seemed to Culver even more exhausted, and even more grimly taut, than it had been an hour before.

The road was a dusty cart-path that rambled footlessly across scrubby, fallow farmland. Shacks and cabins, long ago abandoned, lay along its way. They piled into the jeep, Mannix and Culver in the back, the Colonel in front next to the driver. They hadn't far to go—less than a mile—but the trip felt endless to Culver because the day, by now a fit-

ful carrousel of sleepy sounds, motions without meaning, seemed wildly, almost dangerously abstracted, as if viewed through
drug-glazed eyes or eyes, like those of a mole,
unacquainted with light. Dust billowed past
them as they went. Above them a blue cloud-
less sky in which the sun, pitched now at its
summit, beat fearfully down, augured no
rain for the day, or for the evening. Mannix
said nothing; his silence prompted Culver to
turn and look at him. He was gazing straight
ahead with eyes that seemed to bore through
the Colonel's neck. Tormented beast in the
cul-de-sac, baffled fury, grief at the edge
of defeat—his eyes made Culver suddenly
aware of what they were about to see, and he
turned dizzily away and watched the wreck
of a Negro cabin float past through the
swirling dust: shell-shattered doors and sag-
ging walls, blasted façade—a target across
which for one split second in the fantastic
noon there seemed to crawl the ghosts of the
bereaved and the departed, mourning wraiths
come back to reclaim from the ruins some
hot scent of honeysuckle, smell of cooking,
murmurous noise of bees. Culver closed his

eyes and drowsed, slack-jawed, limp, his stomach faintly heaving.

One boy's eyes lay gently closed, and his long dark lashes were washed in tears, as though he had cried himself to sleep. As they bent over him they saw that he was very young, and a breeze came up from the edges of the swamp, bearing with it a scorched odor of smoke and powder, and touched the edges of his hair. A lock fell across his brow with a sort of gawky, tousled grace, as if preserving even in that blank and mindless repose some gesture proper to his years, a callow charm. Around his curly head grasshoppers darted among the weeds. Below, beneath the slumbering eyes, his face had been blasted out of sight. Culver looked up and met Mannix's gaze. The Captain was sobbing helplessly. He cast an agonized look toward the Colonel, standing across the field, then down again at the boy, then at Culver. "Won't they ever let us alone, the sons of bitches," he murmured, weeping. "Won't they ever let us alone?"

III

That evening at twilight, just before the beginning of the march, Mannix found a nail in his shoe. "Look at it," he said to Culver, "what lousy luck." They were sitting on an embankment bordering the road. The blue dusk was already scattered with stars, but evening had brought no relief to the heat of the day. It clung to them still, damp and stifling, enveloping them like an overcoat. The battalion, over a thousand men, was ready for the march. It stretched out in two files on either side of the road below them for more than a mile. Culver turned and looked down into Mannix's shoe: sure enough, a nail-end had penetrated the lining at the base of the heel, a sharp pinpoint of torture. Mannix inspected the bottom of his big dirty foot. He pulled off a flake of skin which the nail had already worn away. "Of all the lousy luck," he said, "gimme a band-aid."

"It'll wear right through, Al," Culver said, "you'd better get another pair of shoes. Try flattening it out with the end of your bayonet."

Mannix hammered for a moment at the nail and then looked up in exasperation. "It won't go all the way. Gimme that band-aid." A rusty spatter of blood he had picked up at noon was still on the sleeve of his dungarees. He had become nervous and touchy. All that afternoon, after they had come back, he had seemed, like Culver, still shaken by the slaughter, still awed, and rather despondent. Finally, he had alternated moments of remote abstraction with quick outbursts of temper. The shock of the explosion seemed to have set something off in him. His mood had become vague and unpredictable, and he was able to shift from sour, uncommunicative gloom to violent anger in an instant. Culver had never seen him quite so cranky before, nor had he ever seen him so testily at odds with his men, to whom he usually had shown the breeziest good will. All afternoon he'd been after them, nagging, bellowing orders—only to fall suddenly into a profound and brooding silence. As he squatted in the weeds eating his evening meal two hours before, he had hardly said a word, except to murmur—irrelevantly, Culver

thought—that his company "had better goddam well shape up." It puzzled Culver; the
explosion seemed to have stripped off layers
of skin from the Captain, leaving only raw
nerves exposed.

Now he had become fretful again, touchily
alert, and his voice was heavy with impa-
tience. He mumbled as he plastered the
band-aid on his foot. "I wish they'd get this
show on the road. That's the trouble with the
Marine Corps, you always stand frigging
around for half the night while they think up
some grandiose doctrine. I wish to Christ I'd
joined the Army. Man, if I'd have known
what I was getting in for when I went
down to that recruiting office in 1941, I'd
have run off at the door." He looked up
from his foot and down toward the command group nearly at the head of the column.
Three or four officers were clustered together
on the road. The Colonel was among them,
neat, almost jaunty, in new dungarees and
boots. On his head there was a freshly clean
utility cap with a spruce uptilted bill and a
shiny little silver leaf. At his side he wore a
pearl-handled .38 revolver, glistening with

silver inlay. It was, as usual, loaded, though no one knew why, for he was never known to shoot it; the general feeling seemed to be that it was his emblematic prerogative, no more an affectation, certainly, than a visored hat encrusted with gilt, or grenades worn at the shoulder. The pistol—like the swagger stick; the nickname; the quizzical, almost tenderly contemplative air of authority—was part of the act, and to be sure, Culver reflected, the act was less offensive, less imperious than it might be. One simply learned soon to believe that the pistol "belonged," just as the name "Old Rocky" belonged; if such an act finally did no harm, if it only flattered his vanity, was the Colonel to be blamed, Culver asked himself, if he did nothing to mitigate the total impression?

Mannix watched him, too, watched the Colonel toe at the sand, thumbs hooked rakishly in his belt, a thin gentle smile on his face, adumbrated by the fading light: he looked youthful and fresh, nonchalant, displaying the studied casualness of an athlete before the stadium throng, confident of his own victory long before the race begins. Mannix gnawed at the end of a cigar, spat it out viciously. "Look at the little jerk. He thinks he's gonna have us pooped out at the halfway mark—"

Culver put in, "Look Al, why don't you do something about that nail? If you told the Colonel he'd let you ride in—"

Mannix went fiercely on, in a husky whisper: "Well he's not. He's a little sadist, but he's not gonna have Al Mannix crapped out. I'll walk anywhere that son of a bitch goes and a mile further. He thinks H & S Company's been doping off. Well, I'll show him. I wouldn't ask him to ride in if I'd been walking over broken glass. I'll—"

He paused. Culver turned and looked at him. They were both silent, staring at each other, embarrassed by the common understanding of their gaze. Each turned away; Mannix murmured something and began to tie his shoe. "You're right, Al," Culver heard himself saying. It seemed it was almost more than he could bear. Night was coming on. As in a stupor, he looked down the road at the battalion, the men lounging along the embankments with their rifles, smoking and

talking in tired, subdued voices, smoke rising
in giant blue clouds through the dusk, where
swarms of gnats rose and fell in vivacious,
panicky flight. In the swamp, frogs had begun a brainless chorale; their noise seemed
perfectly suited to his sense of complete and
final frustration. It was almost more than he
could bear. So Mannix had felt it, too: not
simply fear of suffering, nor exhaustion, nor
the lingering horror, which gripped both of
them, of that bloody wasteland in the noonday heat. But the other: the old atavism that
clutched them, the voice that commanded,
once again, *you will.* How stupid to think
they had ever made their own philosophy; it
was as puny as a house of straw, and at this
moment—by the noise in their brains of those
words, *you will*—it was being blasted to the
winds like dust. They were as helpless as children. Another war, and years beyond reckoning, had violated their minds irrevocably.
For six years they had slept a cataleptic sleep,
dreaming blissfully of peace, awakened in
horror to find that, after all, they were only
marines, responding anew to the old com-
mands. They were marines. Even if they were

old. Bank clerks and salesmen and lawyers. Even if, right now, they were unutterably tired. They could no more *not* be determined to walk the thirty-six miles than they could, in the blink of an eye, turn themselves into beautiful nymphs. Culver was afraid he wasn't going to make it, and now he knew Mannix was afraid, and he didn't know what to feel—resentment or disgust—over the fact that his fear was mingled with a faint, fugitive pride.

Mannix looked up from his shoe and at the Colonel. "You're goddam right, Jack, we're going to make it," he said. "My company's going to make it if I have to *drag in their bodies.*" There was a tone in his voice that Culver had never heard before.

Suddenly the Colonel's flat voice broke through the stillness: "All right, Billy, let's saddle up."

" 'Tallion saddle up!" The Major's words were eager and shrill, became multiplied down the long mile. "Smoking lamp's out!" The blue cloud dissolved on the air, the gnats descended in a swarm and the voices passed on—*Saddle up, saddle up*—while the bat-

talion rose to its feet, not all at once but in a
steady gradual surge, like rows of corn snap-
ping back erect after the passing of a wind.
Mannix got to his feet, began to sideslip in
a cloud of dust down the embankment toward
his company directly below. It was at the
head of the column, right behind the command group. Culver, moving himself now
down the hill, heard Mannix's shout. It rang
out in the dusk with deliberate authority,
hoarse blunt command: "All right, H & S
Company, saddle up, saddle up! You people
get off your asses and straighten up!" Culver
passed by him on his way to the command
group: he stood surrounded by a cloud of
gnats, hulking enormously above the company, hands balanced lightly on his hips,
poised forward badgering the men like some
obsessed, rakehell Civil War general before a
battle: "All right, you people, we're gonna
walk thirty-six miles tonight and I mean
walk! First man I see drop out's gonna get
police duty for two weeks, and that goes for
everybody. You think I'm kidding you wait
and see. There's gonna be trucks going in for
those that can't make it but I don't want to

see anyone from H & S Company climbing on! If an old man with as much flab as I've got can make it you people can too . . ." There was a note, almost, of desperation in his voice. Culver, passing along the line of bedraggled, mournful-looking men, so few of whom looked like fabled marines, heard the voice rise to a taut pitch close to frenzy; it was too loud, it worried Culver, and he wished to caution him: no longer just admonishing the men to a simple duty, it was the voice of a man wildly fanatic with one idea: to last. "I want to hear no bitching out of you people! Take it easy on the water. You get shinsplints or blisters you see the corpsman, don't come crying to me. When we get in I want to see all of you people . . ." Not because the hike was good or even sensible, Culver thought, but out of hope of triumph, like a chain-gang convict who endures a flogging without the slightest whimper, only to spite the flogger. Culver joined the command group, heard the Colonel say to the Major: "Looks like H & S Company's going to make it *en masse,* Billy." It was just as Culver feared, for although his words were pleasant enough, his face, regarding Mannix for a brief moment, had a look of narrow scrutiny, as if he, too, had detected in the Captain's tone that note of proud and willful submission, rebellion in reverse. But there was no emotion in his voice as he turned quickly, with a glance at his watch, and said, "Let's move out, Billy."

They started out without delay. A jeep, its headlamps lit, preceded them. The Colonel, in the lead, abreast of the Major and just ahead of Culver, plunged off into the deep dust of the road. He walked with a slinky-hipped, athletic stride, head down between his shoulders and slightly forward, arms bent and moving methodically; nothing broke the rhythm of his steps—ruts in the road or the deeply grooved tire tracks—and Culver became quickly amazed, and rather appalled, at the pace he was setting. It was the pace of a trained hiker—determined, unhesitant, much closer to a trot now than a walk—and only a few minutes passed before Culver was gasping for breath. Sand lay thick in the road, hindering a natural step. They had not gone more than a couple of hundred yards; already he felt sweat trickling down his forehead and beneath his arms. For a moment fear surged up in him unnaturally, and a crazy panic. He had been afraid of the march before, but his fear had been abstract and hazy; now so quickly fatigued, in what seemed a matter of seconds, he felt surely (as Mannix had predicted) that he'd be unable to last the first hour. A panicky wash of blood came to his face and he struggled for breath, wanting to cry out—it passed. His mind groped for reason and the terror receded: once he adjusted to the shock of this pace, he realized, he'd be all right. Then the panic went away; as it did so, he found himself breathing easier, freed of that irrational fright. The Colonel pushed ahead in front of him with the absolute mechanical confidence of a wound-up, strutting tin soldier on a table top. Culver, panting a bit, heard his voice, as calm and unwinded as if he were sitting at a desk somewhere, addressed to the Major: "We shoved off at nine on the dot, Billy. We should make the main road at ten and have a break." "Yes, sir," he heard the Major say, "we'll be ahead of the game." Culver made a calculation then:

by the operations map, which he knew so
well, that was three and a half miles—a mile
farther than the regulation distance for an
hour's march. It was, indeed, like running.
Pushing on through the sand, he felt a wave
of hopelessness so giddy and so incompre-
hensible that it was almost like exhilaration
—and he heard a noise—half-chuckle, half-
groan—escape between his labored breaths.
Three and a half miles: the distance from
Greenwich Village almost to Harlem. In his
mind he measured that giddy parade of city
blocks, an exhausting voyage even on wheels.
It was like twisting a knife in his side but he
went on with the mental yardstick—to imagine himself plodding that stretch up the
sandless, comfortably receptive pavements of
Fifth Avenue, past Fourteenth Street and the
bleak vistas of the Twenties and the Thirties,
hurrying onward north by the Library, twenty
blocks more to the Plaza, and pressing still
onward along the green acres of the Park
. . . his thoughts recoiled. Three and a half
miles. In an hour. With more than thirty-
two still to go. A vision of Mannix came
swimming back; Culver stumbled along

after the dauntless Colonel, thinking, Christ on a crutch.

They hastened on. Night had fallen around them, tropic and sudden, lit now, as they descended across a thicket of swampy ground, only by the lights of the jeep. Culver had regained his wind but already his chest and back were awash in sweat, and he was thirsty. He took a vague comfort in the fact that others felt the same way, for behind him he heard canteens being unsnapped from their cases, rattling out of their cups, and the noise, in mid-march, of drinking—a choked, gurgling sound—then, faint to the rear, Mannix's angry voice: "All right, goddammit, I told you people to hold onto your water! Put those goddam canteens back until the break!" Culver, craning his neck around, saw nothing —no Mannix, who had apparently dropped behind—nothing except a shadowy double line of men laboring through the sand, fading off far down the road into the general blackness. To the rear some marine made a joke, a remark; there was laughter and a snatch of song—*on top of old Smo-oky, all covered*

. . . Then Mannix's voice again out of the dark: "O.K. you people can grabass all you want but I'm telling you you'd better save your wind. If you want to talk all the way it's O.K. with me but you're gonna crap out if you do, and remember what I said . . ." His tone had become terse and vicious; it could have been the sound of a satrap of Pharaoh, a galley master. It had the forbidding quality of a strand of barbed wire or a lash made of thorns, and the voices, the song, abruptly ceased, as if they had been strangled. Still his words continued to sting and flay them—already, in this first hour, with the merciless accents of a born bully—and Culver, suddenly angered, had an impulse to drop back and try to make him let up.

"You people close it up now! Dammit, Shea, keep those men closed up there. They fall back they're gonna have to run to catch up! Goddammit, close it up now, you hear me! I mean *you*, Thompson, goddammit you aren't deaf! Close it up! *Close it up*, I said!" So it was that the voice, brutal and furious, continued the rest of the way.

And so it was that those first hours Culver recollected as being the most harrowing of all, even though the later hours brought more subtle refinements of pain. He reasoned that this was because during the first few miles or so he was at least in rough possession of his intellect, his mind lashing his spirit as pitilessly as his body. Later, he seemed to be involved in something routine, an act in which his brain, long past cooperation, played hardly any part at all. But during these early hours there was also the fact of Mannix. Superimposed upon Culver's own fantasies, his anger, his despair (and his own calm moments of rationalization, too) was his growing awareness of what was happening to the Captain. Later, Mannix's actions seemed to become mixed up and a part of the general scheme, the nightmare. But here at first Culver's mind was enough in focus for Mannix's transformation to emerge clearly, even if with the chill, unreal outlines of coming doom—like a man conversing, who might turn around briefly to a mirror and see behind him in the room no longer his familiar friend, but something else—a shape, a ghost, a horror—a wild and threatful face reflected from the glass.

They made the highway at ten o'clock, almost to the minute. When the Colonel looked at his watch and stopped and the Major raised his arm, shouting, "Breather! Ten minutes!" Culver went over to the side of the road and sat down in the weeds. Blood was knocking angrily at his temples, behind his eyes, and he was thirsty enough to drink, with a greedy recklessness, nearly a third of his canteen. He lit a cigarette; it tasted foul and metallic and he flipped it away. His knees and thighs, unaccustomed to so much pounding, were stiff and fatigued; he stretched them out slowly into the dewy underbrush, looking upward at a placid cloud of stars. He turned. Up the road, threading its way through a barrier of outstretched legs and rifles, came a figure. It was Mannix. He was still muttering as he lumbered up and sank down beside him. "Those goddam people, they won't keep it closed up. I have to dog them every minute. They're going to find themselves running the whole way if they don't keep closed up. Gimme a butt." He was breathing heavily, and he passed the back of his hand over his brow to wipe the sweat away.

"Why don't you leave them alone?" Culver said. He gave the Captain a cigarette, which he lit, blowing the smoke out in a violent sort of choked puff.

"Dammit," he replied, coughing, "you *can't* leave them alone! They don't want to make this lousy hike. They'd just as soon crap out on the side and let the trucks haul them in. They'd just as soon take police duty. Man, they're reserves. They don't care who sees them crap out—me, anybody." He fell back with a sigh into the weeds, arms over his eyes. "Fuck it," he said. Culver looked down at him. From the jeep's headlamps an oblong of yellow slanted across the lower part of his face. One corner of his mouth jerked nervously—a distasteful grimace, as if he had been chewing something sour. Exhausted, completely bushed, there was something in his manner—even in repose—which refused to admit his own exhaustion. He clenched his teeth convulsively together. It was as if his own fury, his own obsession now, held up,

Atlas-like, the burden of his great weariness. "Jesus," he murmured, almost irrelevantly, "I can't help thinking about those kids to-day, lying out there in the weeds."

Culver rested easily for a moment, think-ing too. He looked at his watch, with a sink-ing sensation: six of their ten minutes had already passed—so swiftly that they seemed not to have existed at all. Then he said, "Well, for Christ's sake, Al, why don't you let them crap out? If you were getting screwed like these enlisted men are you'd crap out too, you wouldn't care. You don't have to chew them out like you've been doing. Let's face it, you don't really care if they make it. You. Me, maybe. But these guys . . . anybody else. What the hell." He paused, fumbling for words, went on feebly, "*Do* you?"

Mannix rose up on his elbows then. "You're damn right I do," he said evenly. They turned toward the Colonel standing not far away; he and the Major, pointing a flash-light, were bent together over a map. Man-nix hawked something up and spat. His voice became more controlled. "You see that little jerk standing there?" he said. "He thinks he's pulling something on us. Thirty-six miles. *No*body walks that far, stateside. *No*body. We never walked that far even with Edson, last war. See, that little jerk wants to make a name for himself—Old Rocky Templeton. Led the longest forced march in the history of the Corps—"

"But—" Culver started.

"He'd just love to see H & S Company crap out," he went on tensely, "he'd *love* it. It'd do something to his ego. Man, I can see him now"— and his voice lifted itself in a tone of sour mockery— " 'Well, Cap'n Mannix, see where you had a little trouble last night getting your men in. Need a little bit more *esprit*, huh?' " His voice lowered, filled with venom. "Well, screw *him*, Jack. I'll get my company in if I have to carry them on my back—"

It was useless to reason with him. Culver let him go on until he had exhausted his bitter spurt of hatred, of poison, and until finally he lay back again with a groan in the weeds—only a moment before the cry came again: "Saddle up! Saddle up!"

They pushed off once more. It was just a bit easier now, for they were to walk for two miles on the highway, where there was no sand to hinder their steps, before turning back onto the side roads. Yet there was a comfortless feeling at the outset, too: legs cramped and aching from the moment's rest, he walked stooped and bent over, at the start, like an arthritic old man, and he was sweating again, dry with thirst, after only a hundred yards. How on earth, he wondered, gazing up for a second at the dim placid landscape of stars, would they last until the next morning, until nearly noon? A car passed them—a slick convertible bound for the North, New York perhaps—wherever, inevitably, for some civilian pleasure—and its fleet, almost soundless passage brought, along with the red pinpoint of its vanishing taillights, a new sensation of unreality to the night, the march: dozing, shrouded by the dark, its people seemed unaware of the shadowy walkers, had sped unceasingly on, like ocean voyagers oblivious of all those fishy struggles below them in the night, submarine and fathomless.

They plodded on, the Colonel pacing the

march, but slower now, and Culver played
desperately with the idea that the man would,
somehow, tire, become exhausted himself. A
wild fantasia of hopes and imaginings swept
through his mind: that Templeton *would* become fatigued, having overestimated his own
strength, *would* stop the march after an hour
or so and load them on the trucks—like a
stern father who begins a beating, only to
become touched with if not remorse then
leniency, and stays his hand. But Culver
knew it was a hollow desire. They pushed re-
lentlessly ahead, past shadowy pine groves,
fields dense with the fragrance of alfalfa and
wild strawberries, shuttered farmhouses, de-
serted rickety stores. Then this brief civilized
vista they abandoned again, and for good,
when without pause they plunged off again
onto another road, into the sand. Culver had
become bathed in sweat once more; they all
had, even the Colonel, whose neat dungarees
had a black triangular wet spot plastered at
their back. Culver heard his own breath coming hoarsely again, and felt the old panic:
he'd never be able to make it, he knew, he'd
fall out on the side like the old man he was—

but far back to the rear then he heard Mannix's huge voice, dominating the night: "All right, goddammit, move out! We got sand here now. Move out and close it up! Close it up, I say, goddammit! Leadbetter, get that barn out of your ass and close it up! *Close it up, I say!*" They spurred Culver on, after a fashion, but following upon those shouts, there was a faint, subdued chorus, almost inaudible, of moans and protests. They came only from Mannix's company, a muffled, sullen groan. To them Culver heard his own fitful breath add a groan—expressing something he could hardly put a name to: fury, despair, approaching doom—he scarcely knew. He stumbled on behind the Colonel, like a ewe who follows the slaughterhouse ram, dumb and undoubting, too panicked by the general chaos to hate its leader, or care.

At the end of the second hour, and three more miles, Culver was sobbing with exhaustion. He flopped down in the weeds, conscious now of a blister beginning at the bottom of his foot, as if it had been scraped by a razor.

Mannix was having trouble, too. This time when he came up, he was limping. He sat down silently and took off his shoe; Culver, gulping avidly at his canteen, watched him. Both of them were too winded to smoke, or to speak. They were sprawled beside some waterway—canal or stream; phosphorescent globes made a spooky glow among shaggy Spanish moss, and a rank and fetid odor bloomed in the darkness—not the swamp's decay, Culver realized, but Mannix's feet. "Look," the Captain muttered suddenly, "that nail's caught me right in the heel." Culver peered down by the glare of Mannix's flashlight to see on his heel a tiny hole, bleeding slightly, bruised about its perimeter and surrounded by a pasty white where the band-aid had been pulled away. "How'm I going to do it with that?" Mannix said.

"Try beating that nail down again."

"I tried, but the point keeps coming out. I'd have to take the whole frigging shoe apart."

"Can't you put a piece of cloth over it or something?"

"I tried that, too, but it puts my foot off balance. It's worse than the nail." He paused. "Jesus Christ."

"Look," Culver said, "try taking this strip of belt and putting it over it." They debated, operated, talked hurriedly, and neither of them was aware of the Colonel, who had walked over through the shadows and was standing beside them. "What's the matter, Captain?" he said.

They looked up, startled. Hands hooked as usual—Culver wanted to say "characteristically"—in his belt, he stood serenely above them. In the yellow flashlight glow his face was red from exertion, still damp with sweat, but he appeared no more fatigued than a man who had sprinted a few yards to catch a bus. The faint smile hovered at the corners of his lips. Once more it was neither complacent nor superior but, if anything, almost benevolent, so that by the unnatural light, in which his delicate features became fiery red and again now, along the borders of his slim tapering fingers, nearly transparent, he looked still not so much the soldier but the priest in whom passion and faith had made an alloy, at last, of only the purest good intentions; above meanness or petty spite, he was leading a march to some humorless salvation, and his smile—his solicitous words, too —had at least a bleak sincerity.

"I got a nail in my shoe," Mannix said.

The Colonel squatted down and inspected Mannix's foot, cupping it almost tenderly in his hand. Mannix appeared to squirm at the Colonel's touch. "That looks bad," he said after a moment, "did you see the corpsman?"

"No, sir," Mannix replied tensely, "I don't think there's anything can be done. Unless I had a new pair of boondockers."

The Colonel ruminated, rubbing his chin, his other hand still holding the Captain's foot. His eyes searched the dark reaches of the surrounding swamp, where now the rising moon had laid a tranquil silver dust. Frogs piped shrilly in the night, among the cypress and the shallows and closer now, by the road and the stagnant canal, along which danced shifting pinpoints of fire—cigarettes that rose and fell in the hidden fingers of exhausted men. "Well," the Colonel finally said, "well—" and paused. Again the act: indecision before decision, the waiting. "Well," he said, and paused again. The waiting. At that moment—in a wave that came up through his thirst, his throbbing lips, his numb sense of futility—Culver felt that he knew of no one on earth he had ever loathed so much before. And his fury was heightened by the knowledge that he did not hate the man—the Templeton with his shrewd friendly eyes and harmless swagger, that fatuous man whose attempt to convey some impression of a deep and subtle wisdom was almost endearing—not this man, but the Colonel, the marine: that was the one he despised. He didn't hate him for himself, nor even for his brutal march. Bad as it was, there were no doubt worse ordeals; it was at least a peaceful landscape they had to cross. But he did hate him for his perverse and brainless gesture: squatting in the sand, gently, almost indecently now, stroking Mannix's foot, he had too long been conditioned by the system to perform with grace a human act. Too ignorant to know that with this gesture—so nakedly human in the midst of a crazy, capricious punishment which he himself had imposed—he lacerated the Captain by his very touch. Then he spoke. Culver knew what he was going to say. Nothing could have been worse.

"Well," he said, "maybe you'd better ride in on one of the trucks."

If there had been ever the faintest possibility that Mannix would ride in, those words shattered it. Mannix drew his foot away abruptly, as if the Colonel's hand were acid, or fire. "No, sir!" he said fiercely—too fiercely, the note of antagonism, now, was unmistakable— "No, sir! I'll make this frigging march." Furiously, he began to put on his shoe. The Colonel rose to his feet, hooked his thumbs in his belt and gazed carelessly down.

"I think you're going to regret it," he said, "with that foot of yours."

The Captain got up, limping off toward his company, over his retreating shoulder shot back a short, clipped burst of words at the Colonel—whose eyeballs rolled white with astonishment when he heard them— and thereby joined the battle.

"Who cares what you think," he said.

IV

Had the Colonel entertained any immediate
notions of retribution, he held them off, for at
a quarter past four that morning—halfway
through the march, when the first green light
of dawn streaked the sky—Culver still heard
Mannix's hoarse, ill-tempered voice, lashing
his troops from the rear. For hours he had
lost track of Mannix. As for the Colonel, the
word had spread that he was no longer pacing the march but had gone somewhere to the
rear and was walking there. In his misery, a
wave of hope swelled up in Culver: if the
Colonel had become fagged, and was walking
no longer but sitting in his jeep somewhere,
at least they'd all have the consolation of
having succeeded while their leader failed.
But it was a hope, Culver knew, that was ill-
founded. He'd be back there slogging away.
The bastard could outmarch twenty men,
twenty raging Mannixes.

The hike had become disorganized, no
slower but simply more spread out. Culver—
held back by fatigue and thirst and the

burning, enlarging pain in his feet—found himself straggling behind. From time to time he managed to catch up; at one point he discovered himself at the tail end of Mannix's company, but he no longer really cared. The night had simply become a great solitude of pain and thirst, and an exhaustion so profound that it enveloped his whole spirit, and precluded thought.

A truck rumbled past, loaded with supine marines, so still they appeared unconscious. Another passed, and another—they came all night. But far to the front, long after each truck's passage, he could hear Mannix's cry: "Keep on, Jack! This company's walking in." They pushed on through the night, a shambling horde of zombies in drenched dungarees, eyes transfixed on the earth in a sort of glazed, avid concentration. After midnight it seemed to Culver that his mind only registered impressions, and these impressions had no sequence but were projected upon his brain in a scattered, disordered riot, like a movie film pieced together by an idiot. His memory went back no further than the day before; he no longer thought of anything so un-

attainable as home. Even the end of the march
seemed a fanciful thing, beyond all possibility, and what small aspirations he now had
were only to endure this one hour, if just to
attain the microscopic bliss of ten minutes'
rest and a mouthful of warm water. And bordering his memory was ever the violent
and haunting picture of the mangled bodies
he had seen—when? where? it seemed weeks,
years ago, beneath the light of an almost pre-
historic sun; try as he could, to dwell upon
consoling scenes—home, music, sleep—his
mind was balked beyond that vision: the shattered youth with slumbering eyes, the blood,
the swarming noon.

Then at the next halt, their sixth—or seventh, eighth, Culver had long ago lost count
—he saw Mannix lying beside a jeep-towed
water-cart at the rear of his company.
O'Leary was sprawled out next to him, breath
coming in long asthmatic groans. Culver
eased himself painfully down beside them
and touched Mannix's arm. The light of
dawn, a feverish pale green, had begun to ap-
pear, outlining on Mannix's face a twisted
look of suffering. His eyes were closed.

"How you doing, Al?" Culver said, reaching up to refill his canteen.

"Hotsy-totsy," he breathed, "except for my frigging foot. How you making it, boy?" His voice was listless. Culver looked down at Mannix's shoe; he had taken it off, to expose heel and sock, where, soaked up like the wick of a lantern, rose a dark streak of blood.

"Jesus," Culver said, "Al, for Christ sake now, you'd better ride in on a truck."

"Nail's out, sport. I finally stole me a pair of pliers, some radioman. Had to run like hell to catch up."

"Even so——" Culver began. But Mannix had fallen into an impervious silence. Up the road stretched a line of squatting men, Mannix's company. Most were sprawled in the weeds or the dust of the road in attitudes as stiff as death, yet some nearby sat slumped over their rifles, drinking water, smoking; there was a thin resentful muttering in the air. And the men close at hand——the faces he could see in the indecisive light——wore looks of agonized and silent protest. They seemed to be mutely seeking for the Captain,

author of their misery, and they were like
faces of men in bondage who had jettisoned
all hope, and were close to defeat. In the
weeds Mannix breathed heavily, mingling
his with the tortured wheezes of O'Leary,
who had fallen sound asleep. It was getting
hot again. No one spoke. Then a fitful rum-
bling filled the dawn, grew louder, and along
the line bodies stirred, heads turned, gazing
eastward down the road at an oncoming,
roaring cloud of dust. Out of the dust came
a machine. It was a truck, and it passed them,
and it rattled to a stop up in the midst of the
company.

"Anyone crapped out here?" a voice
called. "I got room for ten more."

There was a movement toward the truck;
nearby, half a dozen men got to their feet,
slung their rifles, and began to hobble up the
road. Culver watched them tensely, hearing
Mannix stir beside him, putting his shoe
back on. O'Leary had awakened and sat up.
Together the three of them watched the procession toward the truck: a straggle of limping men plodding as wretchedly as dog-
pound animals toward that yawning vehicle

in the smoky dawn, huge, green, and possessed of wheels—which would deliver them
to freedom, to sleep, oblivion. Mannix
watched them without expression, through in-
flamed eyes; he seemed so drugged, so
dumb with exhaustion, that he was unaware
of what was taking place. "What happened to
the Colonel?" he said absently.

"He went off in a jeep a couple of hours
ago," O'Leary said, "said something about
checking on the column of march."

"What?" Mannix said. Again, he seemed
unaware of the words, as if they—like the
sight of this slow streaming exodus toward
the truck—were making no sudden imprint
on his mind, but were filtering into his con-
sciousness through piles and layers of wool.
A dozen more men arose and began a lame
procession toward the truck. Mannix watched
them, blinking. "What?" he repeated.

"To check the column, sir," O'Leary repeated. "That's what he said."

"He *did?*" Mannix turned with an angry,
questioning look. "Who's pacing the march,
then?"

"Major Lawrence is."

"He *is?*" Mannix rose to his feet, precariously, stiffly and in pain balancing himself not on the heel, but the toe only, of his wounded foot. He blinked in the dawn, gazing at the rear of the truck and the cluster of marines there, feebly lifting themselves into the interior. He said nothing and Culver, watching him from below, could only think of the baffled fury of some great bear cornered, bloody and torn by a foe whose tactics were no braver than his own, but simply more cunning. He bit his lips—out of pain perhaps, but as likely out of impotent rage and frustration, and he seemed close to tears when he said, in a tone almost like grief: *"He* crapped out! *He* crapped out!"

He came alive like a somnambulist abruptly shocked out of sleep, and he lunged forward onto the road with a wild and tormented bellow. "Hey, you people, get off that goddam truck!" He sprang into the dust with a skip and a jump, toiling down the road with hobbled leg and furious flailing arms. By his deep swinging gait, his terrible limp, he looked no more capable of locomotion than a wheel-chair invalid, and it would

have been funny had it not seemed at the
same time so full of threat and disaster. He
pressed on. "Off that truck, goddammit, I say!
Off that truck. Saddle up. Saddle up now, I
say! On your feet!" he yelled. "Get off that
goddam truck before I start kicking you people in the ass!" His words flayed and cowed
them; a long concerted groan arose in the
air, seemed to take possession of the very
dawn; yet they debarked from the truck in
terrified flight, scuttling down like mice
from a sinking raft. "Move the hell out of
here!" he shouted at the truck driver, a
skinny corporal, eyes bulging, who popped
back into the cab in fright. "Get that heap
out of here!" The truck leaped off with a
roar, enveloping the scene in blue smoke and
a tornado of dust. Mannix, with windmilling
arms, stood propped on his toe in the center
of the road, urged the men wildly on. "Saddle up now! Let somebody else crap out O.K.,
but not you people, hear me! Do you hear
me! Goddammit, I mean it! Shea, get those
people moving out up there! You people better face it, you got eighteen more miles to

go . . ." Culver tried to stop him, but they had already begun to run.

Panic-stricken, limping with blisters and with exhaustion, and in mutinous despair, the men fled westward, whipped on by Mannix's cries. They pressed into the humid, sweltering light of the new day. Culver followed; O'Leary, without a murmur, puffed along beside him, while to the rear, with steady slogging footsteps, trailed the remnants of the battalion. Dust billowed up and preceded them, like Egypt's pillar of cloud, filling the air with its dry oppressive menace. It coated their lips and moist brows with white powdery grit, like a spray of plaster, and gave to the surrounding trees, the underbrush and vacant fields, a blighted pallor, as if touched by unseasonable frost. The sun rose higher, burning down at their backs so that each felt he bore on his shoulders not the burden of a pack but, almost worse, a portable oven growing hotter and hotter as the sun came up from behind the sheltering pines. They walked automatically, no longer with that light and tentative step in order to ease the pain in their feet, but with the firm, dogged tread of robots; and if they were all like Culver they had long since parted with a sensation of motion below the hips, and felt there only a constant throbbing pain—of blisters and battered muscles and the protest of exhausted bones.

Then one time Culver saw the Colonel go by in a jeep, boiling along in a cloud of dust toward the head of the column. He caught a glimpse of him as he passed: he looked sweaty and tired, far from rested, and Culver wondered how justified Mannix's outrage had been, assigning to the Colonel that act of cowardice. So he hadn't been pacing the march, but God knows he must have been hiking along to the rear; and his doubts were bolstered by O'Leary's voice, coming painfully beside him: "Old Captain Mannix's mighty pissed off at the Colonel." He paused, wheezing steadily. "Don't know if he's got a right to be that way. Old Colonel ain't gonna crap out without a reason. Colonel's kind of rough sometimes but he'll go with the troops." Culver said nothing. They plodded ahead silently. Culver felt like cursing the Sergeant.

How could he be so stupid? How could he, in the midst of this pain, yield up still only words of accord and respect and even admiration for the creator of such a wild and lunatic punishment? Only a man so firmly cemented to the system that all doubts were beyond countenance could say what O'Leary did—and yet—and yet God knows, Culver thought wearily, he could be right and himself and Mannix, and the rest of them, inescapably wrong. His mind was confused. A swarm of dust came up and filled his lungs. Mannix was screwing everything up horribly, and Culver wanted suddenly to sprint forward—in spite of the effort it took—reach the Captain, take him aside and tell him: *Al, Al, let up, you've already lost the battle.* Defiance, pride, endurance—none of these would help. He only mutilated himself by this perverse and violent rebellion; no matter what the Colonel was—coward and despot or staunch bold leader—he had him beaten, going and coming. Nothing could be worse than what Mannix was doing—adding to a disaster already ordained (Culver somehow sensed) the burden of his vicious fury. At least let up, the men had had enough. But his mind was confused. His kidneys were aching as if they had been pounded with a mallet, and he walked along now with his hands on his waist, like a professor lecturing in a classroom, coattails over his arms.

And for the first time he felt intolerably hot—with a heat that contributed to his mounting fury. At night they had sweated more from exertion; the coolness of the evening had been at least some solace, but the morning's sun began to flagellate him anew, adding curious sharp blades of pain to the furious frustration boiling inside him. Frustration at the fact that he was not independent enough, nor possessed of enough free will, was not *man* enough to say, to hell with it and crap out himself; that he was not man enough to disavow all his determination and endurance and suffering, cash in his chips, and by that act flaunt his contempt of the march, the Colonel, the whole bloody Marine Corps. But he was *not* man enough, he knew, far less simply a free man; he was just a marine—as was Mannix, and so many of the others—and they had been marines, it seemed, all their lives, would go on being marines forever; and the frustration implicit in this thought brought him suddenly close to tears. Mannix. A cold horror came over him. Far down, profoundly, Mannix was so much a marine that it could make him casually demented. The corruption begun years ago in his drill-field feet had climbed up, overtaken him, and had begun to rot his brain. Culver heard himself sobbing with frustration and outrage. The sun beat down against his back. His mind slipped off into fevered blankness, registering once more, on that crazy cinematic tape, chaos, vagrant jigsaw images: Mannix's voice far ahead, hoarse and breaking now, then long spells of silence; halts beside stifling, windless fields, then a shady ditch into which he plunged, feverish and comatose, dreaming of a carnival tent where one bought, from a dozen barrels, all sorts of ice, chipped, crushed, and cubed, in various shapes and sizes. He was awakened by that terrible cry—*Saddle up, saddle up!*—and he set out again. The sun rose higher and higher. O'Leary, with a groan, dropped behind and vanished. Two trucks passed loaded with stiff, green-clad bodies motionless as corpses. The canteen fell off Culver's belt, somewhere, sometime; now he found though, to his surprise, that he was no longer thirsty and no longer sweating. This was dangerous, he recalled from some lecture, but at that moment the young marine vomiting at the roadside seemed more important, even more interesting. He stopped to help, thought better of it, passed on—through a strange crowd of pale and tiny butterflies, borne like bleached petals in shimmering slow-motion across the dusty road. At one point Hobbs, the radioman, cruised by in a jeep with a fishpole antenna; he was laughing, taunting the marchers with a song—*I got romance in my pants*—and he waved a jolly fat hand. A tanager rose, scarlet and beautiful, from a steaming thicket and pinwheeled upward, down again, and into the meadow beyond: there Culver thought, for a brief terrified moment, that he saw eight butchered corpses lying in a row, blood streaming out against the weeds. But it passed. Of course, he remembered, that was yesterday—or was it?—and then for minutes he tried to recall

Hobbs's name, gave up the effort; it was along about this time, too, that he gazed at his watch, neither pleased nor saddened to find that it was not quite nine o'clock, began to wind it with careful absorption as he trudged along, and looked up to see Mannix looming enormously at the roadside.

"Get up," the Captain was saying. He had hardly any voice left at all; whatever he spoke with gave up only a rasp, a whisper. "Get your ass off the deck," he was saying, "get up, I say."

Culver stopped and watched. The marine lay back in the weeds. He was fat and he had a three-day growth of beard. He held up one bare foot, where there was a blister big as a silver dollar and a dead, livid white, the color of a toadstool; as the Captain spoke, the marine blandly peeled the skin away, revealing a huge patch of tender, pink, virgin flesh. He had a patient hillbilly voice and he was explaining softly, "Ah just cain't go on, Captain, with a foot like this. Ah just cain't do it, and that's all there is to it."

"You *can*, goddammit," he rasped. "I

walked ten miles with a nail in my foot. If I can do it you can, too. Get up, I said. You're a marine . . ."

"Captain," he went on patiently, "Ah cain't help it about your nail. Ah may be a marine and all that but Ah ain't no goddam fool . . ."

The Captain, poised on his crippled foot, made a swift, awkward gesture toward the man, as if to drag him to his feet; Culver grabbed him by the arm, shouting furiously: "Stop it, Al! Stop it! Stop it! Stop it! Enough!" He paused, looking into Mannix's dull hot eyes. "Enough!" he said, more quietly. "Enough." Then gently, "That's enough, Al. They've just had enough." The end was at hand, Culver knew, there was no doubt of that. The march had come to a halt again, the men lay sprawled out on the sweltering roadside. He looked at the Captain, who shook his head dumbly and suddenly ran trembling fingers over his eyes. "O.K.," he murmured, "yeah . . . yes"—something incoherent and touched with grief—and Culver felt tears running down his cheeks. He was too tired to think—except: old Al. Mannix. Goddam. "They've had enough," he repeated.

Mannix jerked his hand away from his face. "O.K.," he croaked, "Christ sake, I hear you. O.K. They've had enough, they've had enough. O.K. I heard you the first time. Let 'em crap out! I've did—done—" He paused, wheeled around. "To hell with them all."

He watched Mannix limp away. The Colonel was standing nearby up the road, thumbs hooked in his belt, regarding the Captain soberly. Culver's spirit sank like a rock. Old Al, he thought. You just couldn't win. Goddam. Old great soft scarred bear of a man.

If in defeat he appeared despondent, he retained one violent shred of life which sustained him to the end—his fury. It would get him through. He was like a man running a gauntlet of whips, who shouts outrage and defiance at his tormentors until he falls at the finish. Yet—as Culver could have long ago foretold—it was a fury that was uncontained; the old smoking bonfire had blazed up in his spirit. And if it had been out of control hours ago when he had first defied the Colonel, there was no doubt at all that now it could not fail to consume both of them. At least one of them. Culver, prone on his belly in the weeds, was hot with tension, and he felt blood pounding at his head when he heard the Colonel call, in a frosty voice: "Captain Mannix, will you come here a minute?"

Culver was the closest at hand. There were six more miles to go. The break had extended this time to fifteen minutes—an added rest because, as Culver had heard the Colonel explain to the Major, they'd walk the last six miles without a halt. Another break, he'd said, with a wry weary grin, and they'd never be able to get the troops off the ground. Culver had groaned—another senseless piece of sadism—then reasoned wearily that it *was* a good idea. Probably. Maybe. Who knew? He was too tired to care. He watched Mannix walk with an awful hobbling motion up the road, face screwed up in pain and eyes asquint like a man trying to gaze at the sun. He moved at a good rate of speed but his gait was terrible to behold—jerks and spasms which warded off, reacted to, or vainly tried to control great zones and areas of pain. Behind him most of his men lay in stupefied rows at the edge of the road and waited for the trucks to come. They knew Mannix had finished, and they had crumpled completely. For the last ten minutes, in a listless fashion, he had assembled less than a third of the company who were willing to continue the march —diehards, athletes, and just those who, like Mannix himself, would make the last six miles out of pride and spite. Out of fury. It was a seedy, bedraggled column of people: of hollow, staring eyes and faces green with slack-jawed exhaustion; and behind them the remnants of the battalion made hardly more than two hundred men. Mannix struggled on up the road, approached the Colonel, and stood there propped on his toe, hands on his hips for balance.

The Colonel looked at him steadily for a moment, coldly. Mannix was no longer a simple doubter but the heretic, and was about to receive judgment. Yet there was still an almost paternal reluctance in Templeton's voice as he spoke, slowly and very softly, out of the troops' hearing: "Captain Mannix, I want you to go in on the trucks."

"No, sir," Mannix said hoarsely, "I'm going to make this march."

The Colonel looked utterly whipped; gray bags of fatigue hung beneath his eyes. He seemed no longer to have strength enough to display his odd theatrical smile; his posture was taut and vaguely stooped, the unmistakable bent-kneed stance of a man with blisters, and Culver was forced to concede—with a sense of mountainous despair—that he *had* made the march after all, somewhere toward the rear and for legitimate reasons of his own, even if Mannix now was too blind, too outraged, to tell. *Goddam,* Culver heard himself moaning aloud, *if just he only hadn't made it,* but he heard the Colonel go on coolly: "Not with that foot you aren't." He glanced down. The Captain's ankle had swollen to a fat milky purple above the top of his shoe; he was unable to touch his heel to the ground even if he had wanted to. "Not with that foot," he repeated.

Mannix was silent, panting deeply—not as

if taken aback at all, but only as if gathering wind for an outburst. He and the Colonel gazed at each other, twin profiles embattled against an escarpment of pines, the chaste blue sky of morning. "Listen, Colonel," he rasped, "you ordered this goddam hike and I'm going to walk it even if I haven't got one goddam man left. You can crap out yourself for half the march—" Culver wanted desperately, somehow, by any means to stop him— not just because he was pulling catastrophe down on his head but because it was simply no longer worth the effort. Couldn't he see? That the Colonel didn't care and that was that? That with him the hike had had nothing to do with courage or sacrifice or suffering, but was only a task to be performed, that whatever he was he was no coward, he had marched the whole way—or most of it, any idiot could see that—and that he was as far removed from the vulgar battle, the competition, which Mannix had tried to promote as the frozen, remotest stars. He just didn't care. Culver strove, in a sick, heaving effort, to rise, to go and somehow separate them, but

Mannix was charging on: "You run your troops. Fine. O.K. But what's all this about crapping out—"

"Wait a minute, Captain, now—" the Colonel blurted ominously. "For your information—"

"*Fuck* you and your information," said Mannix in a hoarse, choked voice. He was almost sobbing. "If you think—"

But he went no further, for the Colonel had made a curious, quick gesture—stage-gesture, fantastic and subtle, and it was like watching an old cowboy film to see the Colonel's hand go swiftly back to the handle of his pistol and rest there, his eyes cool and passionate and forbidding. It was a gesture of force which balked even the Captain. Mannix's face went pale—as if he had only just then realized the words which had erupted so heedlessly from his mouth—and he said nothing, only stood there sullen and beaten and blinking at the glossy white handle of the pistol as the Colonel went on: "For your information, Captain, you aren't the only one who made this march. But I'm not *interested* in your observations. You quiet down now,

hear? You march in, see? I order you confined to your quarters, and I'm going to see
that you get a court-martial. Do you understand? I'm going to have you tried for gross
insubordination. I'll have you sent to Korea.
Keep your mouth shut. Now get back to your
company!" He was shaking with wrath; the
hot morning light beat with piety and with
vengeance from his gray, outraged eyes. "Get
back to your men," he whispered, *"get back
to your men!"*

Then he turned his back to the Captain and
called down the road to the Major: "All
right, Billy, let's saddle up!"

So it was over, but not quite all. The last
six miles took until past noon. Mannix's per-
petual tread on his toe alone gave to his gait
a ponderous, bobbing motion which resem-
bled that of a man wretchedly spastic and
paralyzed. It lent to his face too—whenever
Culver became detached from his own misery
long enough to glance at him—an aspect of
deep, almost prayerfully passionate concentration—eyes thrown skyward and lips fluttering feverishly in pain—so that if one did
not know he was in agony one might imagine

that he was a communicant in rapture, offering up breaths of hot desire to the heavens. It was impossible to imagine such a distorted face; it was the painted, suffering face of a clown, and the heaving gait was a grotesque and indecent parody of a hopeless cripple, with shoulders gyrating like a seesaw and with flapping, stricken arms. The Colonel and the Major had long since outdistanced them, and Culver and Mannix walked alone. When the base came into sight, he was certain they were not going to make it. They trudged into the camp. Along the barren, treeless streets marines in neat khaki were going to lunch, and they turned to watch the mammoth gyrating Captain, so tattered and soiled—who addressed convulsive fluttering prayers to the sky, and had obviously parted with his senses. Then Mannix stopped suddenly and grasped Culver's arm. "What the hell," he whispered, "we've made it."

v

For a long while Culver was unable to sleep.
He had lain naked on his bed for what seemed
hours, but unconsciousness would not come;
his closed eyes offered up only vistas of endless roads, steaming thickets, fields, tents—
sunshine and darkness illogically commin-
gled—and the picture, which returned to his
mind with the unshakable regularity of a
scrap of music, of the boys who lay dead beneath the light of another noon. Try as he
could, sleep would not come. So he dragged
himself erect and edged toward the window,
laboriously, because of his battered feet; it
took him a full minute to do so, and his legs,
like those of an amputee which possess the
ghost of sensation, felt as if they were still in
motion, pacing endless distances. He lowered
himself into a chair and lighted a cigarette.
Below, the swimming pool was grotto-blue,
a miniature of the cloudless sky above, lit
with shapes of dancing light as shiny as silver
dimes. A squad of sunsuited maidens, officers' wives, splashed at its brink or ate ice-

cream sundaes on the lawn, and filled the
noontime with their decorous sunny laughter.
It was hot and still. Far off above the pines,
in the hot sunlight and over distant peace
and civilization, brewed the smoky and
threatful beginnings of a storm.

Culver let his head fall on his arm. Yes,
they had had it—those eight boys—he
thought, there was no doubt of that. In mindless slumber now, they were past caring,
though diadems might drop or Doges surren-
der. They were ignorant of all. And that they
had never grown old enough to know anything, even the tender miracle of pity, was
perhaps a better ending—it was hard to tell.
Faint warm winds came up from the river,
bearing with them a fragrance of swamp and
pine, and a last whisper of air passed through
the trees, shuddered, died, became still; suddenly Culver felt a deep vast hunger for
something he could not explain, nor ever
could remember having known quite so ach-
ingly before. He only felt that all of his life
he had yearned for something that was as
fleeting and as incommunicable, in its beauty,
as that one bar of music he remembered, or

those lovely little girls with their ever joyful,
ever sprightly dance on some far and fantastic lawn—serenity, a quality of repose—he
could not call it by name, but only knew that,
somehow, it had always escaped him. As he
sat there, with the hunger growing and blos-
soming within him, he felt that he had hardly
ever known a time in his life when he was
not marching or sick with loneliness or
afraid.

And so, he thought, they had all had it, in
their various fashions. The Colonel had had
his march and his victory, and Culver could
not say still why he was unable to hate him.
Perhaps it was only because he was a different kind of man, different enough that he was
hardly a man at all, but just a quantity of
attitudes so remote from Culver's world that
to hate him would be like hating a cannibal,
merely because he gobbled human flesh. At
any rate, he had had it. And as for Mannix—
well, *he'd* certainly had it, there was no doubt
of *that*. Old Al, he thought tenderly. The man
with the back unbreakable, the soul of pity—
where was he now, great unshatterable ves-
sel of longing, lost in the night, astray at

mid-century in the never-endingness of war?

His hunger faded and died. He raised his head and gazed out the window. Over the pool a figure swan-dived against the sky, in cruci- fied, graceless descent broke the water with a lumpy splash. A cloud passed over the day, darkening the lawn with a moment's somber light. The conversation of the girls became subdued, civilized, general. Far off above the trees, on the remotest horizon, thunderheads bloomed, a squall. Later, toward sundown, they would roll landward over a shadowing reach of waves, borne nearer, ever more darkly across the coast, the green wild deso- lation of palmetto and cypress and pine—and here, where the girls pink and scanty in sun- suits would slant their tar-black eyes sky- ward in the gathering night, abandon pool and games and chatter and with shrill cries of warning flee homeward like gaudy scraps of paper on the blast, voices young and lovely and lost in the darkness, the onrushing winds. One thing, Culver thought, was certain—they were in for a blow. Already there would be signals up and down the coast.

Abruptly he was conscious of a dry,

parched thirst. He rose to his feet, put on a robe, and hobbled out into the hallway toward the water cooler. As he rounded the corner he saw Mannix, naked except for a towel around his waist, making his slow and agonized way down the hall. He was hairy and enormous and as he inched his way toward the shower room, clawing at the wall for support, his face with its clenched eyes and taut, drawn-down mouth was one of tortured and gigantic suffering. The swelling at his ankle was the size of a grapefruit, an ugly blue, and this leg he dragged behind him, a dead weight no longer capable of motion.

Culver started to limp toward him, said, "Al—" in an effort to help him along, but just then one of the Negro maids employed in the place came swinging along with a mop, stopped, seeing Mannix, ceased the singsong little tune she was humming, too, and said, "Oh my, you poor man. What you been doin'? Do it hurt?" Culver halted.

"Do it hurt?" she repeated. "Oh, I bet it does. Deed it does." Mannix looked up at her across the short yards that separated them, silent, blinking. Culver would remember this:

the two of them communicating across that chasm one unspoken moment of sympathy and understanding before the woman, spectacled, bandannaed, said again, "Deed it does," and before, almost at precisely the same instant, the towel slipped away slowly from Mannix's waist and fell with a soft plop to the floor; Mannix then, standing there, weaving dizzily and clutching for support at the wall, a mass of scars and naked as the day he emerged from his mother's womb, save for the soap which he held feebly in one hand. He seemed to have neither the strength nor the ability to lean down and retrieve the towel and so he merely stood there huge and naked in the slanting dusty light and blinked and sent toward the woman, finally, a sour, apologetic smile, his words uttered, it seemed to Culver, not with self-pity but only with the tone of a man who, having endured and lasted, was too weary to tell her anything but what was true.

"Deed it does," he said.

ABOUT THE AUTHOR

WILLIAM STYRON was born in Newport. News, Virginia. He served three years in the United States Marine Corps, and after the war, returned to complete his studies at Duke University.

Lie Down in Darkness, William Styron's first novel, appeared in 1951. For that initial work, he was awarded the Prix de Rome of the American Academy of Arts and Letters. Two years later his short novel, *The Long March,* was published, followed by *Set This House on Fire* (1960) and *The Confessions of Nat Turner* (1967).

Mr. Styron, his wife and four children live in Roxbury, Connecticut.